Acting Edition

I0741578

Seared

by Theresa Rebeck

FOR PRODUCTION INQUIRIES

UNITED STATES AND CANADA
info@concordtheatricals.com
1-866-979-0447

UNITED KINGDOM AND EUROPE
licensing@concordtheatricals.co.uk
020-7054-7298

Each title is subject to availability from Concord Theatricals Corp., depending upon country of performance. Please be aware that SEARED may not be licensed by Concord Theatricals Corp. in your territory. Professional and amateur producers should contact the nearest Concord Theatricals Corp. office or licensing partner to verify availability.

This work is published by Samuel French, an imprint of Concord Theatricals Corp.

No one shall make any changes in this title(s) for the purpose of production. No part of this book may be reproduced, stored in a retrieval system, scanned, uploaded, or transmitted in any form, by any means, now known or yet to be invented, including mechanical, electronic, digital, photocopying, recording, videotaping, or otherwise, without the prior written permission of the publisher. No one shall share this title(s), or any part of this title(s), through any social media or file hosting websites.

For all inquiries regarding motion picture, television, online/digital and other media rights, please contact Concord Theatricals Corp.

MUSIC AND THIRD-PARTY MATERIALS USE NOTE

Licensees are solely responsible for obtaining formal written permission from copyright owners to use copyrighted music and/or other copyrighted third-party materials (e.g. artworks, logos) in the performance of this play and are strongly cautioned to do so. If no such permission is obtained by the licensee, then the licensee must use only original music and materials that the licensee owns and controls. Licensees are solely responsible and liable for clearances of all third-party copyrighted materials, including without limitation music, and shall indemnify the copyright owners of the play(s) and their licensing agent, Concord Theatricals Corp., against any costs, expenses, losses and liabilities arising from the use of such copyrighted third-party materials by licensees. For music, please contact the appropriate music licensing authority in your territory for the rights to any incidental music.

IMPORTANT BILLING AND CREDIT REQUIREMENTS

If you have obtained performance rights to this title, please refer to your licensing agreement for important billing and credit requirements.

SEARED was first produced by the Williamstown Theater Festival on July 25, 2018, in Williamstown, Massachusetts. The production was directed by Moritz von Stuelpnagel, with set design by Tim Mackabee, costume design by Tilly Grimes, lighting design by David Weiner, and sound design by Palmer Heferan. The cast was as follows:

HARRY	Hoon Lee
RODNEY	W. Tré Davis
MIKE	Michael Esper
EMILY	Krysta Rodriguez

SEARED had its Off Broadway debut at the The Robert W. Wilson MCC Theater Space/Susan and Ronald Frankel Theater in New York City on October 28, 2019. The production was directed by Moritz von Stuelpnagel, with set design by Tim Mackabee, costume design by Tilly Grimes, lighting design by David Weiner, and sound design by Palmer Heferan. The Production Stage Manager was Rachel Gross.The cast was as follows:

HARRY	Raul Esparza
RODNEY	W. Tré Davis
MIKE	David Mason
EMILY	Krysta Rodriguez

CHARACTERS

HARRY – Forty-five. Any ethnicity. Harry is obstreperous, demanding, kind, self-destructive, passionate and brilliant. A difficult but worthy genius.

RODNEY – Twenty-one. Black. Rodney is a kid of the neighborhood, smart, loyal, Harry's acolyte. He has a deep and honest love for his mentor.

MIKE – Mid-40s. It is important that Mike and Harry are the same age as they came up through the ranks of the restaurant industry as peers. Any ethnicity. Mike is devoted to Harry and his exacting standards and bends over backwards to help Harry achieve his vision, but he is a realist.

EMILY – Twenty-seven. Any ethnicity. Emily is charming, sexual, and extremely and unapologetically capable. She knows how to operate.

SETTING

The small, slightly run-down kitchen of a restaurant that will either slide into oblivion or leap ahead into success. When the story begins, there are many eccentricities in the way the place is held together.

TIME

The recent past, or the present.

AUTHOR'S NOTES

There is a lot of overlap, which only gets more pronounced as the stakes get crazier. Where the overlap begins in a line is indicated with a forward slash (/). In all other places feel free to let it rip, of course keeping in mind the information the audience needs to hear.

Some of the cooking must happen onstage, but not all of it necessarily has to.

ACT ONE

Scene One

(The sound of oil sizzling, the smell of garlic. As the lights come up we see:)

*(**HARRY**, forty-five, a big guy in every way. He wears a white chef's apron, and red bandana tied on his head.)*

(He dominates a clean but cluttered kitchen. Large six-burner stove, pots, drawers, a large refrigerator.)

HARRY. *(To himself.)* Fennel where's the fennel?

*(**RODNEY** enters. He is twenty-one, African American, skinny, good natured, on the move. Well dressed in a sort of way. He sticks a meal order next to the two already in place at **HARRY**'s eye level.)*

Where's the fennel?

RODNEY. I don't know.

*(**RODNEY** leaves. While **HARRY** keeps an eye on the frying garlic, he grabs a plate of portobello mushrooms and slices them efficiently. Drops butter into another pan, takes a piece of white fish off a platter and*

dredges it in flour. Chops asparagus, looks for fennel among the vegetables piled on the counter.)

*(**MIKE** enters.)*

HARRY. You know where the fennel is?

MIKE. You put it back in the crisper.

HARRY. Why would I do that?

MIKE. I don't know Harry you just do it I need the balsamic?

HARRY. It's where it always is. What's this?

*(**HARRY** is reading a ticket. **RODNEY** reenters, goes for the chilled salad plates. **HARRY** holds the slip up and **RODNEY** barely pauses to read it.)*

RODNEY. Scallops, that's scallops.

HARRY. We don't have scallops tonight. Snapper.

(He flips it, reaches for the pasta cooker, shakes it, and pulls finished pasta out of the water, plates it.)

RODNEY. You know when we'll have 'em next?

HARRY. I'll keep an eye out for 'em, they didn't look so good this morning. Tell 'em the snapper or the lamb, the pasta's good too.

RODNEY. What's in the pasta?

HARRY. Sage and fennel, ricotta cheese, pancetta, grilled onions.

RODNEY. What's it called?

HARRY. Pasta.

RODNEY. I think she might be a vegetarian.

HARRY. She wanted scallops!

RODNEY. Yeah, she said they were really good.

HARRY. Tell her everything's good.

RODNEY. *(Sad.)* She was pretty excited about those scallops.

> *(But* **RODNEY** *heads back out, passing* **MIKE**, *who is on his way back in with another ticket.)*

MIKE. There's a big spender at the four top in the window. TWO bottles of the Masi Amarone, wants me to open it up and let it breathe while they start with Prosecco.

HARRY. That's not a big spender, that's just a drunk showing off for a new girlfriend.

> *(***HARRY** *finishes the plated snapper and then the pasta. He hands them both to* **MIKE**.*)*

MIKE. They've got a table full of appetizers, gnocchi, prosciutto, bruschetta –

> *(***HARRY** *studies the ticket.)*

HARRY. Yeah okay.

> *(He reaches up, tosses sliced homemade bread into a toaster on top of the oven.* **MIKE** *finishes the garnish on the pasta and wipes the edge of the plated snapper. He tastes it.)*

MIKE. Wow, what is that?

HARRY. Cinnamon.

MIKE. No, not that.

HARRY. I put a little ancho chili in it.

MIKE. Ancho chili.

> *(***MIKE** *heads out as* **RODNEY** *heads back in.)*

RODNEY. She wants the scallops.

HARRY. We don't have scallops.

> (**HARRY** *is collecting fresh gnocchi from a nearby bowl, ready to toss it into the pasta cooker.*)

RODNEY. She's really sad.

HARRY. She hasn't eaten anything yet, she's probably just hungry.

RODNEY. I have to offer her something else, she doesn't want anything that's on the menu.

HARRY. Then she should go to another restaurant.

RODNEY. I'm not telling her to go to another restaurant. That's rude. I mean, that's rude. She comes here all the time. She loves it here. You don't want her to go to another restaurant.

> (**MIKE** *comes back in.*)

HARRY. I don't know what to say. I don't have any scallops.

RODNEY. Come on, Harry, you're making my job harder. Everyone wants scallops so the first thing I have to do is disappoint them and tell them I don't have any scallops.

MIKE. I'll run across the street to the Key Food.

HARRY. No no no

MIKE. I've told you a million times no one cares if the scallops are fresh.

HARRY. Are you kidding?

MIKE. They can't tell the difference; they don't care.

HARRY. Cold disgusting mealy

MIKE. They don't.

HARRY. Watery frozen

MIKE. Stop it you know how to cook a scallop and I can get them fresh at the meat counter those guys at the Key Food

HARRY. The Key Food

MIKE. Those are professional guys and their fish department

HARRY. I'm not having this discussion

MIKE. All the scallops are flash frozen on the boat.

HARRY. I'm not cooking a frozen scallop!

(He finishes plating his appetizers.)

MIKE. Rodney, take my four top in the window.

HARRY. He's got his own tables.

MIKE. And now he's got mine too. Because I'm going to the fucking Key Food and I'm buying some fucking scallops.

*(**MIKE** heads for the back door.)*

HARRY. I won't cook them.

MIKE. We have a regular customer

HARRY. Offer her the pork belly sliders, I have one order left from last night.

RODNEY. She doesn't want pork belly, she wants scallops.

HARRY. Then sell it.

*(**RODNEY** goes back out as **HARRY** goes to the refrigerator and finds the last order of pork bellies. He doesn't look at **MIKE**. He continues to cook. **MIKE** hangs in the doorway. **RODNEY** returns.)*

RODNEY. She's fine with the pork bellies.

HARRY. I know she's fine with the pork bellies. And she hasn't even tasted them yet.

> *(He tosses them into a skillet on the stovetop. Starts chopping vegetables.* **RODNEY** *looks back and forth between* **MIKE** *and* **HARRY**.*)*

RODNEY. You still want me to take your four top in the window?

> *(A moment of silence. Neither man answers.* **RODNEY** *just takes the appetizers and goes back out to the floor.)*

> *(***HARRY** *continues to cook.* **MIKE** *looks out into the alleyway.)*

MIKE. You can't say you're not going to serve the scallops. People come here, okay I told you this morning this was going to happen when *New York Magazine* came out with that little blurb about your scallops. We were written up in *New York Magazine* for the fucking scallops. You can't just choose not to serve the scallops.

> *(***HARRY** *just keeps cooking.)*

We're not a big enough establishment to be *(Pronounced "eye-diosyncratic.")* idiosyncratic.

HARRY. *(Pronouncing it correctly.)* Idiosyncratic.

MIKE. You know what I'm saying.

HARRY. Don't you fucking call me idiosyncratic.

MIKE. Oh my god that is the nice word when you're in a mood like this.

HARRY. I'm not in a mood; I'm in the middle of a dinner rush.

MIKE. It's too small a restaurant to have a dinner rush.

HARRY. We got sixteen setups and people lining up on the sidewalk.

MIKE. That's my point. People are lining up for the scallops.

HARRY. They are lining up for the food.

MIKE. When the food critics at *New York Magazine* / call our ginger lemongrass scallops exquisite

HARRY. When those fucking food critics – "our"? Did you just call them "our" scallops?

MIKE. Harry, don't. We're in the middle of a dinner rush.

HARRY. I thought we were "too small" for a dinner rush.

MIKE. That's not what I

HARRY. You just said it, not thirty seconds ago. I said we were in the middle of a dinner rush, I got work to do here.

> *(And he is,* **HARRY** *continues to cook and plate as he argues.)*

MIKE. We are both back here and the kid too, trying to make this work

> *(***RODNEY*** *comes in, a little panicked.)*

RODNEY. Two more snappers, they want to split the gnocchi.

HARRY. No takers on the lamb? I hate Park Slope. Aside from the vegetarians who love pork belly, all the meat eaters have just laid down and died. People are carnivores, we're carnivores, we eat each other alive for sport. Have they not noticed this? Fucking scallops.

RODNEY. They wanted the scallops, seriously six people have been asking about the scallops.

> *(There is a pause at this.)*

MIKE. I'm going to go get them.

HARRY. Do not go get them. I'm warning you. Do not go get them.

(Blackout.)

Scene Two

(**HARRY** *cleaning the kitchen. He pours hot
water into a French press coffee maker, then
lets the coffee steep while he moves dishes
into the sink.* **RODNEY** *comes in, yawning.
He wears a hoodie sweatshirt which he takes
off while* **HARRY** *pours him a cup of coffee.*
RODNEY *roots through his backpack, pulls
out a greasy brown paper bag, opens it, and
gives* **HARRY** *a doughnut. Both of them drink
their coffee and eat their doughnuts.)*

RODNEY. So how many of those snappers you end up
  making last night?

HARRY. Sixteen, seventeen, I can't remember. We ran out.

RODNEY. I never was a fan of snapper.

HARRY. No?

RODNEY. It just bores me. Even the way you cook it.

HARRY. I think I'm insulted.

RODNEY. No no you know I love what you make.

HARRY. Except when it's snapper.

RODNEY. Yeah but I never like snapper. That's what I'm
  saying. It's like lima beans, no matter what you do to a
  lima bean, I can't eat it.

> (*As they continue speaking,* **RODNEY** *reaches
> into his pocket and takes out a wad of bills.
> He counts off ten, and hands them to* **HARRY**,
> *who pockets them.)*

HARRY. You don't like lima beans.

RODNEY. Can't eat them.

HARRY. You're Black.

RODNEY. What's that got to do with it?

HARRY. I don't know it just seems

RODNEY. That is so racist.

HARRY. Food isn't racist.

RODNEY. I'm not saying food's racist, I'm saying you're racist.

HARRY. I'm not racist.

RODNEY. Lima beans. Black eyed peas. Fried chicken.

HARRY. Everybody likes fried chicken.

RODNEY. Okra. Greens.

HARRY. This is a good regional menu.

RODNEY. I'm Black so I got to like greens.

HARRY. Do you?

RODNEY. Greens is fine.

HARRY. Macaroni and cheese?

RODNEY. Everybody likes macaroni and cheese.

HARRY. Not everybody likes all macaroni and cheese.

RODNEY. You should do a macaroni and cheese.

HARRY. There's not really any compelling reason to.

RODNEY. It's delicious would be the compelling reason.

HARRY. Doughnuts are delicious, I'm not making a doughnut.

RODNEY. Why not?

HARRY. It's somebody else's issue. I have no curiosity about doughnuts. I enjoy eating a doughnut, I find myself compelled, there is no question things are circling the doughnut the way the doughnut circles the hole, but beyond that, look. I'm going to give you some wisdom here. This is worth knowing. There is not an infinite number of things that you can do in your life. There is infinity, no question, but its circles get smaller, not larger. And that's not a bad thing. I mean honestly there are at least twenty ways to cook a couple of asparagus tips, so you do the math, asparagus, garlic, scallions, butter, heavy cream, sage leaves, rosemary, cracked pepper, butter, sugar snap peas, prosciutto, olive oil, basil, soy sauce, butter. Like, there's a lot of, already, you wouldn't call it noise, because that carries the wrong – because things open, they open for each other, and for you, which is why butter – it's frankly impossible to explain how butter does what it does. But there is an infinite number of doors which are opened with butter. And that's as much as any one person who is trying to communicate with a larger cosmos can handle. So you have to make choices.

> *(He finishes his doughnut.* **RODNEY** *starts to laugh.)*

RODNEY. Communicate with the cosmos.

> *(***HARRY*** *laughs too.)*

HARRY. Yeah, okay. Maybe I will try to make a doughnut someday. It's just hard to imagine why I'd bother when you can get a really good one for what does this cost, a dollar?

RODNEY. Three dollars.

HARRY. *(Stunned.)* Three dollars?

RODNEY. Yeah, the place up on Flatbush. These are three dollar donuts. Actually, three-fifty.

HARRY. You paid three-fifty for these donuts? Each one?

RODNEY. Well, come on, someone says this donut is worth three-fifty, you got to know what it tastes like. Be real. And you got to admit, this is an excellent donut.

HARRY. Three-fifty worth?

RODNEY. I would say yes.

HARRY. Would you go back though? Like tomorrow morning, or next week?

RODNEY. Well, three-fifty for a donut, that's not something that should be encouraged. There's something a little, it's against nature. I read this thing one time, in a magazine, they got some restaurant in Manhattan where you can pay a thousand dollars for an omelet.

HARRY. I heard about that.

RODNEY. I mean, come on. That's just, it's hard to say what that is.

HARRY. They put a ton of caviar on it, apparently. That'll jack up the price of anything.

RODNEY. A thousand bucks?

HARRY. It's got lobster too.

RODNEY. That costs nothing.

HARRY. Don't tell them.

RODNEY. A thousand dollars for an omelet.

HARRY. I actually think it's two thousand dollars now.

RODNEY. You ever taste it?

HARRY. It costs two thousand dollars.

>   (**RODNEY** *is amazed, thinking about that.*
>   **HARRY** *starts to set up for his prep.*)

RODNEY. You should've made those scallops.

HARRY. I'm not revisiting this.

RODNEY. I'm just telling you. I like you.

HARRY. You like me so you're going to tell me how to run my kitchen, that's terrific.

RODNEY. Look. Those scallops are, you know how good they are.

HARRY. All my food is good.

RODNEY. Yeah but Harry don't talk to me like I'm an idiot. That food critic showed up, you didn't give him everything else you know how to do.

HARRY. He wasn't actually a food critic. He was a fucking stringer for the Best Bets column.

RODNEY. My point being

HARRY. "Best Bets."

RODNEY. There was a picture of your scallops in *New York Magazine*. He called you a hidden jewel, Harry.

HARRY. What is a hidden jewel?

RODNEY. You know what a hidden jewel is.

HARRY. I know what an idiot is, too.

RODNEY. You think the guy who called you a "hidden jewel" is an idiot.

HARRY. I think

RODNEY. You wanted to impress that guy! You found out he was out there, you sent him the scallops!

HARRY. I also sent him the gnocchi with the sage butter.

RODNEY. Which he also liked

HARRY. AND the sardines

RODNEY. The sardines got too many bones in them, I don't care what anyone says.

HARRY. *(Overlap.)* All of it for free, we feed these fuckers for free

RODNEY. That's not the point Harry, the point is that you served the scallops because you wanted to impress this guy and you did impress him and he liked your cooking, that's what you wanted and now you're acting all like it's crazy that people want to eat the scallops. You're being kind of a jerk honestly.

HARRY. I'm not being a jerk

RODNEY. You're being a little bit of a jerk. I'm telling you that as a friend. We work hard you know, me and Mike.

HARRY. Nobody works harder than me

RODNEY. *(He's been through this.)* I didn't say we worked harder than you but honestly we are all busting our asses here and we caught a break, man! The dude from *New York Magazine* comes here and gives us a great little pop on the Best Bets page

HARRY. I don't give a shit what some moron in *New York Magazine* says. I don't need *New York Magazine* to tell me I know how to cook a scallop.

RODNEY. Then why did you serve it to that guy? Why didn't you give him the worst food you know how to cook? Why didn't you give him a carrot, like, a carrot on a plate. Who cares why. What I know is, you didn't serve him that. You gave him your scallops. Which no one else knows how to cook a scallop like you. I been watching you for a year now, you're doing things to those scallops no one else has ever thought of and it's awesome, it's a total, he was right to say you got to have the scallops. And you are not right to say he shouldn't have written that. Because people should come here for the scallops man, and you should serve them to them.

HARRY. I'm not going to spend the rest of my life cooking scallops.

RODNEY. Not the rest of your life. Just the next couple months. People are coming here, they want scallops.

HARRY. I'm not feeling the scallops.

RODNEY. You don't have to feel them, you just have to cook them.

HARRY. Says who.

RODNEY. Mike.

HARRY. Mike doesn't tell me what to do.

RODNEY. Does he know that?

HARRY. Rodney, listen to me. You don't tell me what to do. Mike doesn't tell me what to do. Nobody tells me what to do.

>*(A **WOMAN** enters the kitchen. She is **EMILY**, twenty-seven, bright, confident, personable, enthusiastic. Well dressed in a way that is a little out of place. **MIKE** comes in behind her.)*

EMILY. Hello.

HARRY. Hello?

EMILY. I'm Emily.

MIKE. *(Bright.)* This is Emily! Emily Lowes.

EMILY. I'm such a fan.

HARRY. Oh, thanks.

EMILY. I was here last night.

HARRY. Were you?

EMILY. My friends and I saw the mention in *New York Magazine.*

HARRY. Okay.

EMILY. So we came down to see what all the fuss was about. Let me tell you something. You did not disappoint.

HARRY. Great.

EMILY. I was just telling Mike, your restaurant is sensational. I think it's amazing what you two have done with such a small space.

HARRY. You actually don't need a lot of space to cook a decent...

EMILY. Oh no no of course that's not what I mean. Maybe it is what I mean. I'm so used to seeing places that have much more extensive resources, not just in terms of staff, and money –

HARRY. This is Rodney.

EMILY. Hello, Rodney.

RODNEY. *(Unsure.)* Hey.

EMILY. This is the whole place. It's amazing. Well, you're amazing. My meal last night was impeccable.

HARRY. I'm glad you liked it.

EMILY. We had the gnocchi, superb, prosciutto, the bruschetta to start, I had the pasta which was extraordinary and my friend had the lamb.

HARRY. I like the lamb.

EMILY. He felt it was undercooked but he was wrong, I had a piece, it was like butter and the rosemary infusion was just sublime, I've never seen anyone do it that way, what do you

HARRY. *(Bemused.)* It's not really an infusion, it's a rub.

EMILY. A rub!

> *(She has taken out her cell phone and is texting.)*

HARRY. Yeah, you crumble it with the cracked pepper and –

EMILY. Amazing.

> *(**HARRY** looks at **MIKE**.)*

HARRY. Well, thanks for stopping by.

MIKE. Emily and I have been talking.

HARRY. Okay.

MIKE. She'd like to help us.

HARRY. Do we need help?

EMILY. You are of course right to ask that question because you're a genius chef and your restaurant is a complete neighborhood jewel and a wonderful achievement.

HARRY. Everything's so great in your universe.

EMILY. *(Laughing.)* Not everything, no. Too many things are not great at all. Which is why I have a job.

HARRY. "Helping."

EMILY. Well, yes.

> (**HARRY** *looks at* **RODNEY**. *This whole situation stinks.)*

MIKE. Rodney, run down the block to Victor's and get a squeegee, would you? The front windows are a mess.

RODNEY. We got a squeegee somewhere.

MIKE. That thing's a piece of junk, get a new one.

> *(He hands him a twenty.)*

RODNEY. Yeah, okay.

> *(He looks at* **HARRY**, *who looks back at him, shrugs.* **RODNEY** *pockets the twenty and splits.)*

MIKE. Emily is a consultant.

HARRY. Wow, a consultant. Okay. And can I ask, are we consulting right now, Emily?

EMILY. I hope so.

HARRY. Okay.

MIKE. I think she's worth listening to.

HARRY. So you go ahead and listen to her all you want. I have to prep.

MIKE. I'm not asking you to do anything more than have a conversation

HARRY. You are already doing so much more than asking.

MIKE. With a knowledgable person about how we might

HARRY. You bring this total stranger into my kitchen

MIKE. Capitalize on this moment. We have been working for a long time Harry

HARRY. And you don't ask, you tell me that I'm supposed to suddenly be "consulting" with some girl –

MIKE. She has a lot of good ideas. And you are not just going to blow through this and refuse to discuss this. It's my restaurant, too. And I'm well within my rights to say we have to at least have a conversation.

　　　(A beat.)

HARRY. You want to have a conversation?

MIKE. Yes.

HARRY. Because I think we are having a conversation.

MIKE. Not you and me. You and me and her.

HARRY. You want me to have a conversation with her.

MIKE. I am going to insist upon it.

HARRY. Oh you insist.

MIKE. Harry.

HARRY. Okay, you know. Okay. I hear you. Emily, I apologize. This caught me a little unawares.

EMILY. I'm sure! It's caught me unawares.

HARRY. You're a consultant.

EMILY. I am.

HARRY. What do you consult about, Emily?

EMILY.   A lot of things. I work with a lot of different organizations, small businesses, start-ups, entrepreneurs, largely in the food service industry, helping them focus their assets and their goals so that they can maximize their potential and get what they want.

HARRY. Wow. You help people get what they want?

EMILY. I do.

HARRY. Yeah, but the problem is, I have what I want. So I don't need anybody to help me get what I want. Sorry.

MIKE. *(Abrupt.)* I don't have what I want.

> *(That stops the room.* **HARRY** *looks at him, pissed.* **MIKE** *doesn't look at him.)*

Let me get you a seat, Emily.

> *(***MIKE*** *goes back into the restaurant.* **EMILY** *smiles at* **HARRY***, who doesn't smile back.* **MIKE** *returns with a chair, offers it to* **EMILY***. She sits, puts down her bag, and starts making notes on her cell.)*

EMILY. My understanding is that when you two started this place what was it, two, two and a half years ago, you had limited funds but an excess of talent.

> *(Smiles at* **HARRY***.)*

And a determination to work outside the system.

HARRY. Where did you get this understanding?

MIKE. From me. We sat down, this morning.

HARRY. This morning.

MIKE. We got to talking last night. She really enjoyed the meal, and she gave me her card. So then I called her this morning, and we had breakfast. I thought she had some interesting ideas so I asked her if she'd come over here and tell you about them.

HARRY. Well, that's just – great.

> *(There is a pause as **HARRY** stews about that.
> **EMILY** makes a decision.)*

EMILY. I should come back.

MIKE. No! This is a good time!

EMILY. Actually, I think the two of you could go over the things we discussed and you can get back to me. There is no pressure from my end. Your restaurant is terrific and sometimes I get excited and moving too fast is not always the right idea.

HARRY. Or never the right idea.

> *(The anxiety spikes. Everyone starts speaking
> quickly.)*

MIKE. This isn't too fast; we've been talking about how do you expand a place that has sixteen setups

HARRY. "Too fast" by definition is "too" "fast".

MIKE. The only way to make a profit is to

HARRY. *(To **EMILY**.)* Thank you we appreciate your interest in butting your nose in

MIKE. Have a great night every night of the week! And even then we're barely breaking even

HARRY. But I think I got this covered

EMILY. *(To **HARRY**.)* I honestly had no intention of stepping on any toes

MIKE. I don't want you to leave. We have to have this conversation with him. The things you were talking about are really encouraging.

HARRY. I am not having a conversation with you with a third person in the room who I don't know.

MIKE. Well, you're going to know her because I'm not burying my head in the sand about this and neither are you.-09

HARRY. "Burying my head in the sand"

MIKE. As soon as they raise the rent on this place we got nothing

HARRY. You've been moaning about the rent for as long as we've been here.

MIKE. Because it's too high already and that issue is going to get worse not better and it's not just your livelihood on the line here, Harry.

HARRY. I refuse to be bullied into taking on another partner because you

MIKE. Bullied? If anyone is a "bully" in this situation / it would not be me.

HARRY. Have some sort of neurotic need to grow, expand, make more of a cultural splash

MIKE. I don't see anything wrong with any of those things, it's not "neurotic" it's more like just acknowledging / what people are already saying, we're bursting at the seams here and that mention in *New York Magazine* has put us on the map

HARRY. It's all fucking American capitalist bullshit, nothing matters unless there are people talking about you on the fucking internet, / these people, these PEOPLE

MIKE. Which is a good thing because we cannot survive like this WE CANNOT SURVIVE!

(He silences **HARRY** *with that one.* **HARRY** *stares at him.)*

HARRY. Survive. We're doing fine.

MIKE. I am worn to the bone. Every night I am here till all hours and then I am up again at six, to meet you at the fish market only to be told there is nothing worthy of you to cook in the vast oceans of sea creatures which lap the shores of our mighty city. We go to the best butcher in Brooklyn, the finest cuts of meat barely meet your begrudging acceptance. We go to the markets I spend the day arguing with you about the bounty of America which is flung at your feet by the farmers and bakers and cheese makers, all of them brilliant, none of it good enough for your genius.

HARRY. It's my job to create beautiful food. You can't do that without the right ingredients. That's just reality.

MIKE. Reality doesn't work.

HARRY. Yes, that is true; reality is alarmingly challenging in every way and at all times, there is not much to recommend reality in general. People also fall into this category of things one might prefer to avoid in every way. But we don't avoid them, because the fuckers are everywhere, like reality, and the only way to deal with them and it, is with a pound of butter and some decent ingredients. There is a way to negotiate this impossible situation with regard to – all of it – and that is to make reality your own, put it in a fucking kitchen and I don't know, make friends with it. Acknowledge it. Accept it. Honor it. You just said reality doesn't work. But that's not strictly the case. People don't work. Reality works in very small doses.

MIKE. Not here it doesn't.

HARRY. This is the only place it does work.

MIKE. I cannot handle an existential debate if I'm not drunk.

HARRY. This isn't a debate.

MIKE. *(Still debating.)* We could lose everything.

HARRY. Which is my point.

MIKE. Good we agree.

HARRY. We couldn't disagree more.

MIKE. This isn't an abstract situation, it's just not abstract, it's not theoretical.

HARRY. We agree on that at least.

MIKE. Our profit margin is too small. As soon as the rent goes up, we lose everything. That is reality.

HARRY. Reality is food.

MIKE. That is a specious thing to say, Harry! I have given everything I am to you and your fucking food.

HARRY. You gave me

MIKE. You know I did.

HARRY. That is classic.

MIKE. Harry

HARRY. This whole thing is standing on me. My talent, my work.

MIKE. My money.

HARRY. If that's what's important to you

MIKE. It is important to me! It is! I don't know how to live with no money!

EMILY. Can I just interrupt for a second?

HARRY. No.

MIKE. Yes.

EMILY. I cannot tell you how wonderful it is to hear you guys having this conversation. So many partnerships find themselves at the first real impasse and nobody has the language or, more importantly, the courage to really get down to the issues at hand and that's it. It's over. Most people honestly don't know how to face conflict. But you do. It's an honor, honestly, to listen to you two argue. It's so pure.

HARRY. *(To* **MIKE***.)* I really don't want to talk to her.

EMILY. You don't have to talk to me. I'm not here to hold your hand and make you feel better. You're not the kind of man who needs that. What's more this isn't about what you need, or what Mike needs. It's about the container for everyone's needs. It's about the universe which allows things to grow. Right now you both are living in a world that isn't big enough, which is why you're fighting over resources. I'm here to take that problem off your shoulders. Let me assure you, the world is big enough. I can make it big enough.

(Lights shift.)

Scene Three

(A week later. **RODNEY**, **EMILY** *and* **MIKE** *in the kitchen,* **EMILY** *has a large box.* **RODNEY** *has a portable blackboard which he is wiping clean.)*

EMILY. I have a surprise for Harry.

MIKE. What kind of surprise?

EMILY. A good surprise.

RODNEY. You know, he is not really big on surprises.

EMILY. You are so funny. Can someone help me?

*(***MIKE*** goes to take the box from her.)*

MIKE. I think if we keep our adjustments out of the kitchen for now that might...

RODNEY. Adjustments?

EMILY. I know that's what we planned. This is just an opportunity that came up and I thought it would be crazy not to give it a go.

RODNEY. Plans?

MIKE. Not plans. Thoughts is more

RODNEY. Okay, for sure, I just wasn't sure 'cause Harry didn't mention that you all were moving ahead with adjustments.

EMILY Where are your dishes?

RODNEY. Oh, our dishwasher guy, he's always late. I mean they show up. Just usually late.

(She starts to move the toaster oven.)

MIKE. Maybe we shouldn't move that.

EMILY. What is it?

MIKE. It's a toaster oven.

EMILY. A toaster oven?

MIKE. When we were just starting Harry would come in and prep everything and then it was ready and all he had to do was heat it up in a toaster oven.

EMILY. You got in the Best Bets column at *New York Magazine* reheating food in a toaster oven. Doesn't that just go to show. They don't know as much as they think they do.

(*She unplugs it.*)

MIKE. It doesn't mean that.

EMILY. You're superstitious about critics?

MIKE. I'm superstitious about toaster ovens. Harry has made some beautiful meals in that toaster oven.

EMILY. You can't possibly control the heat properly. I'll talk him into a sous vide.

RODNEY. If I was you I would leave the toaster oven alone.

EMILY. You know what? It's charming. It completely adds character.

(*She starts to reorganize the counter space.*)

RODNEY. Well he doesn't use it anymore. It's mostly someplace to like just put things. Sauces, or anchovies.

EMILY. He keeps anchovies in here? Adorable. Just adorable.

RODNEY. Whoa. I just never heard anyone call Harry "adorable" before.

> (**HARRY** *enters, with a bag of donuts. He is checking out what's behind him, in the dining room.*)

HARRY. Okay so somebody's delivered a truckload of tables and chairs, who wants to explain to the idiot here where we're supposed to put them?

EMILY. On the sidewalk.

HARRY. You need a permission slip.

MIKE. We have one.

HARRY. We have one?

MIKE. Yes.

HARRY. Those take months.

MIKE. No they don't. We went to the Public Works office on Friday to apply for a table and chairs permit, they turned it around in a few hours.

HARRY. Well that was nice of them.

MIKE. Emily knew somebody.

HARRY. I bet she did.

EMILY. They are really excited down there for people to make this move.

HARRY. They are not!

(**RODNEY** *leaves to check out tables and chairs.*)

EMILY. Of course they are! My god, anyone who really feels they've got the clientele to support an expansion, trust me, local government is not going to stand in the way of that.

HARRY. Local government stands in the way of everything it possibly can. What planet are you living on.

EMILY. I'm living on the planet that gave you a tables and chair permit the day you applied for one.

HARRY. I didn't apply for anything.

EMILY. I know. We did it for you. So stop complaining.

HARRY. *(Looking around.)* Jesus Christ what's going on here.

EMILY. You're getting a makeover.

HARRY. Oh fuck you.

MIKE. That's not

HARRY. I told you

MIKE. Harry you agreed that we could / try a few things. Just a few things.

HARRY. There would be no fucking makeovers of my kitchen – who moved the toaster oven?

MIKE. You haven't used the toaster oven

HARRY. Don't tell me what I do and what I don't do. Where are my plates?

MIKE. That's just José. He's late again.

HARRY. Where are my knives?

EMILY. Your knives are where they always are.

HARRY. So why don't I see them?

EMILY. We just thought you might want to see these first.

> *(She pushes a box forward. He looks at what's in the box.)*

They are new ones. For anyone who wants to use them. Or not. This one is a Misono 440 Molybdenum Santoku. Look at that. Korin's Deba knife. A Takamura. Kikuichi.

> *(**HARRY** takes one of the knives, looks at it. He points it at her. She laughs and takes a step back.)*

HARRY. Who's paying for all this?

EMILY. I have friends who like to do me favors.

HARRY. So this is free?

EMILY. It's an investment.

HARRY. What do your friends want for their investment?

EMILY. They want us to succeed.

HARRY. Okay. Okay, great. I'm glad so many people I don't know have my best interest at heart, that's always an encouraging thing to think about the human race who up to now have not actually impressed me with their spirit of camaraderie toward itinerant chefs. So how many new place settings you think you're going to squish out there on our three square feet of sidewalk?

EMILY. There's more room than that.

HARRY. How many more set ups, Emily, are you thinking you're going to put out there.

EMILY. *(A beat.)* Twelve.

HARRY. Twelve!

MIKE. Eight.

HARRY. The restaurant only seats sixteen.

EMILY. The restaurant seats twenty, and the sidewalk will seat twelve.

MIKE. You said eight.

HARRY. Over my dead body.

MIKE. Okay, I do think that's a little

EMILY. It's ambitious.

HARRY. You're talking about adding twice as many people.

EMILY. Not quite that many

HARRY. Four plus twelve I think you said, that's sixteen last time I checked.

*(**RODNEY** reenters.)*

RODNEY. Wow.

EMILY. You won't be booking all those tables; at least not at

HARRY. This is fucked.

MIKE. Harry. You agreed.

HARRY. I didn't agree to this.

MIKE. You agreed that we could try out a few of her ideas, you agreed you would at least try.

HARRY. Twice as many tables is not an idea.

MIKE. If it doesn't work

HARRY. This is fucked.

MIKE. We will rethink but we cannot just keep walking away from the problem!

RODNEY. If you add that many tables, you going to hire more people?

EMILY. Well –

HARRY. I am not sharing my kitchen.

MIKE. Whoa, first of all it's not "your" kitchen, last time I checked I'm still the only person who put real money in place.

HARRY. Don't even start to argue this point, Mike, this was, the whole reason, the whole REASON

MIKE. Was me. It was my money. You may not want to admit it now but my money is

HARRY. Please don't say real. Money is not real! Food is real!

MIKE. My money is real at least it was when I cleaned out my bank account

RODNEY. Whoa

EMILY. Guys guys guys / we are going to do this one step at a time.

HARRY. *(Overriding both of them.)* This olive oil is real, this KNIFE is real.

MIKE. Oh my god I am so within my rights and I am so tired. My money made this place happen.

HARRY. Money is legal tender. It's nothing. It's a symbol for value, and it's paper and you can't eat it. You can't wear it; you can't get high on it; it is the biggest fraud perpetrated on the history of mankind and every one of us is betting our LIVES on the complete and utter fabrication of money! Your money is more real than my life, my talent, my time, my patience, my love, everything that is essential and passionate about what I have and what I do is nothing compared to your money and just stop, I know you are not going to, I'm not saying it's you saying this. That's the worst thing about it, it's not even you who is saying this to me, it's everything else and what you are is just compromised, not compromised, it's subsumed by the fact of your money. It's not even current money, it's two years ago there was some money and now it's evaporated, so it's even the memory of money that we're talking about. The memory of your money from two years ago owns everything, in this equation, it at least owns your imagination because what else is she doing here? The imagined future where there is more imagined money is more real to you than the most essential – a human being, the eye, the hand, a glass of wine, friendship, the belief in in making something real out of –

You'd give all this up for money? And not even very much money? Capitalism? You'd give this up for some fucked up American idea that money is GOOD?

(There is a dangerous silence.)

MIKE. You listen to me. I am well aware that you are a brilliant hothead and that you can talk almost as well as you can cook but you know what? I don't give a shit.

MIKE. *(To* **EMILY**.*)* I'm going to go set up those tables.

(He goes. After a moment, **EMILY** *goes with him.)*

(Blackout.)

Scene Four

*(The end of the shift. **HARRY**, alone, is finishing up the last few dinners.)*

(He sautés broccoli in olive oil, seasons it. Tosses it. He opens the oven and takes out a bubbling casserole. Reaches into it carefully and plates short ribs. He reaches over and finds a pot of soft polenta.)

*(**RODNEY** enters, carrying an armful of dirty dishes. He puts them in the sink.)*

RODNEY. I need my short ribs.

*(**HARRY**, behind him, spoons soft polenta onto a plate, then from a saucepan spoons mushrooms onto it. He grabs a bottle of balsamic vinegar, drizzles it over the polenta, tosses the broccoli. **RODNEY** reaches for the plated short ribs and bumps the casserole with his hand, pulls back as soon as he touches it.)*

Fuck. That's hot, man. That's hot.

HARRY. Who said it wasn't.

RODNEY. Dammit, Harry. It's right in the middle of the counter you got it right in the middle of the

HARRY. I didn't tell you to touch it.

RODNEY. Fuck you.

HARRY. Do not start on me man.

*(**MIKE** enters, with more dishes. He puts them on the counter.)*

MIKE. The party of six wants dessert.

RODNEY. Fuck them.

MIKE. Just show them, it's on the board.

RODNEY. They probably want cappuccinos, too.

HARRY. What's this?

>   (**MIKE** *has put a new ticket on the stovetop.*)

MIKE. A table of two, they just walked in.

HARRY. We're closed.

MIKE. I just sat them.

HARRY. Go unseat them.

MIKE. I'm not doing that. It's just appetizers.

HARRY. I don't give a shit. It's eleven-thirty. I've served
sixty-two short ribs and four hundred sides of gnocchi
in five hours.

MIKE. Rodney go talk them through

RODNEY. I'm with Harry.

MIKE. The dessert menu

>   (**EMILY** *enters, cheerful, upbeat.*)

EMILY. What a night! Oh my god people are still showing
up, it's eleven-thirty at night. It's amazing and Harry
oh my GOD the short ribs were impeccable from start
to finish. Everyone is talking about it. Now I just have
to get you to make those scallops. You guys must be
exhausted, I'm going to take care of the dessert for that
party of six.

>   (*She goes.*)

HARRY. (*Pissed.*) She works here now?

MIKE. She's just helping out.

HARRY. That's what she was doing before.

MIKE. Look, it's late and we're all tired.

HARRY. We're all TIRED because we've been cranking out twice as many meals.

RODNEY. Yo, what's she going to want for that? I have to share my tips with her, too?

MIKE. She's not going to want your tips.

RODNEY. Good.

MIKE. Nobody wants your tips.

RODNEY. Yeah, okay.

> *(But there is now something unspoken.* **HARRY** *watches* **RODNEY**, *turns back to the sink.)*

MIKE. What kind of tips you pull in tonight?

RODNEY. I did pretty good.

MIKE. So this new arrangement suits you?

RODNEY. Well I don't want to work this hard every night.

MIKE. But you're okay with the money? You don't see it as something that's a big nothing that's corrupting your soul?

RODNEY. This kind of change? Once or twice a week I wouldn't say no.

MIKE. That's very broad-minded of you.

> *(**EMILY** enters, still chipper. She goes to the refrigerator and starts to plate desserts.)*

EMILY. They're going to split the ginger maple cheesecake and the chocolate mousse.

HARRY. That's not enough for six people.

EMILY. I was thinking of comping them some biscotti.

HARRY. That's nice of you.

EMILY. Well, it's the end of the evening anyway and they're looking at a seven hundred dollar check.

MIKE. It's a great idea.

(**HARRY** *is starting to plate the cookies.*)

EMILY. I got it! They want to meet the chef.

(**HARRY** *looks at her.*)

HARRY. They "asked" to meet the chef.

EMILY. Yes they did in fact. One of them is some sort of restaurant fanatic and he wants to talk to you.

HARRY. He wants to give me notes?

EMILY. He wants to tell you you're good! What's wrong with that? It's been a long day, you all did amazing but especially you, Harry, you doubled your output in one night and if anything the food was better than ever. Go out there and take a bow.

HARRY. I have a ticket.

EMILY. *(Adorable.)* Come on. Harry, you know that the whole story on this place is that there's a mad scientist in the kitchen making the most astonishing food in Brooklyn. You have to get out there and let them get a look at you and prove that you are not an epic lunatic, you're a handsome, charming, eccentric genius. Say hello to your fans. They are going to be so nice to you. Everyone does it as you well know and you have to do it too. Come on. Come talk to them. I know you know how to talk.

(*She turns and goes. After a moment,* **HARRY** *follows, reluctant.*)

(**MIKE** *and* **RODNEY** *look at each other.*)

RODNEY. Seriously. Is she going to share in the tips?

MIKE. No.

RODNEY. You sure? Because she's like, taking over.

MIKE. We needed to make some changes.

RODNEY. I can't believe her. She's like so annoying and then everyone does what she says. How does she do that?

MIKE. She knows what she's talking about.

RODNEY. And people gave her all that stuff? The tables and chairs and the permit and the knives. They just gave it all to her like for free.

MIKE. Nothing's for free.

RODNEY. So what's your deal with her?

MIKE. You know what? My deal with her is with her, and my deal with you is with you.

RODNEY. Yeah, okay.

> *(He drifts over to the door to spy through to the dining room.)*

Does Harry know what her deal is?

MIKE. Okay. You want to walk down this road, let's walk down this road. When you asked if you had to share your tips with her too, what did you mean by that?

RODNEY. What?

MIKE. Do I have to share my tips with her "too." "Her too." It's what's you said.

RODNEY. So?

MIKE. Don't play with me.

RODNEY. I'm not.

MIKE. What does that, what does that

RODNEY. Just does she share the tips.

MIKE. Are you sharing your tips with him?

> *(There is a slight pause at this as **RODNEY**
> tries to figure out how to answer it.)*

Oh, Jesus God above.

RODNEY. Oh come on.

MIKE. How long?

RODNEY. Are you actually asking me that?

MIKE. Yes, I am.

RODNEY. You didn't know.

MIKE. You know I didn't.

RODNEY. People decide what they want to know. So you
can decide not to know? But that doesn't mean that
you didn't.

> *(Pissed now, **RODNEY** goes and starts plating
> a few salads.)*

MIKE. Let's pretend I don't know.

RODNEY. Okay yeah we can pretend that.

MIKE. So I'm an idiot, I don't know, that's why I'm asking.
Are you sharing your tips with Harry?

RODNEY. Yeah.

MIKE. How long?

RODNEY. Since I started! That was the deal. It was the
deal with Andre, it was the deal with Ramon.

MIKE. But he arranged this with you, it was between the
two of you. He told you not to tell me.

RODNEY. It's a restaurant. People share tips. He works like
an animal, why shouldn't he share the tips?

MIKE. How much?

RODNEY. Half.

MIKE. God damn it.

RODNEY. Hey could you –

MIKE. I didn't know.

>   *(Then.)*

Don't give him any more of your tips.

RODNEY. Are you serious?

MIKE. Yes, I'm serious.

RODNEY. So, you're going to make him work twice as hard and then you're going to pay him half the money?

MIKE. He doesn't like money.

RODNEY. No, he likes money.

MIKE. Money is for capitalist sellouts.

RODNEY. You get tips. I get tips. Why shouldn't Harry get tips, he works harder than anybody.

MIKE. Just don't give him any more of your tips.

RODNEY. Man. We were doing good.

MIKE. And now we're doing better.

>   *(**HARRY** returns, goes to the stove, checks that last ticket. **EMILY** is with him and hangs in the doorway.)*

EMILY. Did you watch? Did you watch?

RODNEY. I saw some.

HARRY. *(Off the ticket.)* Anybody do anything about these appetizers?

RODNEY. Yeah.

(**RODNEY** *takes his plates and goes.*)

EMILY. *(To* **MIKE.***)* He's fantastic with the customers. He's a rock star. You were hilarious. That whole speech about hating money, is pure genius. Just like the food. So fantastically real. Which is let's face it in this city that doesn't come along every day.

HARRY. I'm glad you like how real I am.

EMILY. Oh my god, what a day. You guys are amazing. When Mike asked me to take this on I thought well we will see, we will see. Because a lot of people think they're ready for change but trust me very few people are ready for change. You guys, you don't really have to change anything, you just have the open the doors and let the air in. You are going to make a lot of money.

HARRY. I don't care about money.

EMILY. I know I know I know.

> *(She laughs and picks up a bottle of open wine.)*

What's this, Barolo?

MIKE. The four top in the window didn't finish it.

> *(She smells it, pours.)*

EMILY. Well it's opened up beautifully. Here's to you, Harry. I am so glad this day is over.

HARRY. Yeah me too because I'm fucking beat, and I got to get up at five a.m. and get to the fish market.

EMILY. Tomorrow's Saturday, the fish markets are closed.

HARRY. My guy comes in from Long Island to hit the farmer's market in Prospect Park, I got to get to him before the yuppies do.

EMILY. Come on this was such a big day!

HARRY. And now it's almost tomorrow.

EMILY. Don't serve fish tomorrow.

HARRY. I'm sorry, don't

EMILY. How about some sort of Asian fusion thing, how come you don't have that on the menu?

HARRY. Because I'm from New Jersey.

EMILY. Okay. Catfish! Bluefish. Some delicious bottom feeder, there's always plenty of them out there.

HARRY. Sad but true.

EMILY. And I bet you do an amazing fried catfish.

HARRY. My catfish is good, yes.

EMILY. So tomorrow, fried catfish on the menu which means you can sleep in. You've earned it.

> *(She hands him a glass of wine.* **HARRY** *thinks about that, takes the glass, drinks. She looks for another glass.)*

HARRY. Mike, you want some?

MIKE. Have you been stealing Rodney's tips?

> *(***HARRY*** *turns and looks at him.* **EMILY** *is pouring out the rest of the wine into hers and* **HARRY***'s already full glasses.)*

HARRY. *(A beat.)* What kind of question is that?

MIKE. It's a question I want an answer to.

> *(There is a pause.)*

HARRY. Rodney and I share his tips, sure.

MIKE. You "share" his tips. It was his idea.

HARRY. Is he complaining?

MIKE. I'm complaining. I'm the one complaining.

HARRY. Why?

EMILY. Everyone shares tips.

MIKE. You need to stay out of this.

HARRY. Why does she need to stay out of this? She's already in every other corner of our business.

EMILY. You guys. We still have two tables out in the dining room.

HARRY. Well maybe you'd better go take care of them.

EMILY. *(Bright.)* I will.

(At door.)

Just, whatever this is? Remember today was a big success and you're tired and if you ask me this could wait.

HARRY. I think you were told to stay out of this.

EMILY. I was! Just – try to keep the volume down.

*(She goes. **MIKE** and **HARRY** square off.)*

MIKE. We are partners.

HARRY. Is that right.

MIKE. For two and a half years I've been trying to put us into the black enough, to make just enough money to make a little bit of my investment back.

HARRY. Which is why you get to keep your tips.

MIKE. My tips go into the till! My tips are part of the income that goes into the rent and the upkeep and the endless soul-sucking pursuit of the best cuts of meat and the impossible scallops. You pull a salary.

HARRY. Neither one of us is getting rich, Mike, that's not why we did it!

MIKE. You're getting a lot richer a lot faster than I am.

HARRY. Half that kid's tips are hardly making me rich!

MIKE. Then why are you taking them?

HARRY. Everybody shares tips.

MIKE. Then why was it a secret. Why didn't you tell me. Why didn't we pool all the tips.

HARRY. What's your point.

MIKE. You are not entitled to that kid's tips. You pull a salary.

HARRY. You pull a salary.

MIKE. We had a deal.

HARRY. Is this like an ethical question?

MIKE. Yeah it's an ethical question.

HARRY. Because here's another ethical question: Why did you hire a consultant without consulting me?

MIKE. I hired a consultant because this restaurant is broke, I'm broke and you would be broke too, if you weren't stealing tips from that kid who works his ass off for you and adores you.

HARRY. *(Snapping.)* I am broke, I just don't mind being broke as long as it means I get to do whatever I want.

MIKE. Well you're about to be more broke. Let's see if you mind that. Because if you had been as broke as me, all along, maybe you'd understand why we can't stay this broke. But you don't understand, yet, because you're living off that kid's tips. Because

HARRY. I got it I got it.

> *(A beat.)*

MIKE. Good. Because we're all going to sink or swim, together.

HARRY. That's not what we've been doing?

MIKE. Apparently not.

(*Then.*)

Listen to me.

We've been working our asses off for two and a half years and it could all go away in a heartbeat if we don't figure something out. You want to go back and work in somebody else's kitchen? It was killing you and you were pissing everybody off and it just was a fucking waste and we have a moment right now. We've earned it and I don't know what to do with it. All I know how to do with that thing in *New York Magazine* is cut it out and laminate it and stick it in the window. She knows more. She just – knows more.

(*A beat.*)

HARRY. So how much are we paying her?

MIKE. We're not paying her anything. Yet.

HARRY. All of this is on spec.

MIKE. I'll let her explain it.

(*He goes back into the dining room.* **HARRY** *is alone for a moment, drinking wine.*)

(*He looks around. Picks up one of those knives, finds an onion, slices through it. It goes through like butter. He thinks about that. Finishes off the wine. Then goes at the onion full throttle, shredding it for a long moment. He holds it up, looks at it.*)

(**EMILY** *stands in the doorway, watching.* **HARRY** *looks over at her.*)

EMILY. The Kikuichi. I might have guessed.

HARRY. What's it worth?

EMILY. Retail, I have no idea. Each one is handcrafted. They'd love it if you'd endorse it.

HARRY. Is that the deal on all of them?

EMILY. Well, you pick one. The rest go back.

HARRY. Who do they go back to?

EMILY. Does it matter?

> *(A beat.)*

Just think about it. The Kikuichi, I mean. It doesn't have to be the Kikuichi. Try them all. We can take this one step at a time.

HARRY. You don't take anything one step at a time.

EMILY. Well, no. Do you?

> *(She laughs at him. He considers her. Blackout.)*

End Act One

ACT TWO

Scene One

(*Night. A new stainless steel table on wheels, decked out with implements and the newest kitchen gadgetry, stands alongside the other equipment.*)

(**HARRY** *stands in the middle of the kitchen. He is alone. Bowls of vegetables, herbs, bottles of oil, ramekins, as well as a huge piece of salmon, surround him.*)

(*He starts to chop. Chops a jalapeño into smaller and smaller pieces. Then shallots, one after another.*)

(*In the middle of this process, he turns, picks up a gorgeous pan, looks at it, then puts it on the stove, turns it on. He picks up a bottle of olive oil, drenches the pan in it.*)

(*He looks into the ramekins, finds the one he wants, pours it into a bowl and whisks. Finds another, pours it in, whisks.*)

(*Throws in some spices, tastes it. Sets it aside.*)

(Picks up the giant piece of salmon. Sets it in front of him and slices a piece off, turns and drops it in the oil.)

(Picks up another pan and turns the burner on. While that heats up he finds a tin of canned sardines. Opens it, throws the sardines into the pan. Goes back to the cluttered ingredients, reaches in and finds a small jar. He pops it open, looks around for an implement. Finds what he is looking for – a tiny fork. He forks a caper and tastes it. It tastes all right. He puts a few of them in with the sardines. Then tosses in jalapeño and onions.)

(Turns the salmon.)

(He opens the oven, pulls out a plate. He sets it on the counter and then opens a steamer next to the oven, reaches in with tongs, pulls out asparagus spears, tosses them into another pan, drizzles them with oil and starts to sear them.)

(There are lots of things on the stove now. He starts to move between them, tasting, turning, stirring, and then finally putting the whole plate together.)

(He sets it on the counter, turns everything off. He looks at the plated salmon for a moment, then he takes a bite. He thinks about it, and then dumps it into the trash can next to the sink.)

(Blackout.)

Scene Two

> *(The next day.* **HARRY** *is at the stove, watching* **EMILY** *eat a piece of salmon.)*

EMILY. It's amazing.

HARRY. It's getting there.

EMILY. Where is it supposed to go?

HARRY. No, it's good. I'm saying it's good. It's a good start.

EMILY. It's fantastic.

> *(Focused, she reaches for another forkful. Flirting, he pulls the plate away, steps in and kisses her. She returns the kiss, then pulls away.)*

Think of what you want to call it, because it's going on the menu tonight.

> *(That's a surprise.)*

HARRY. Tonight?

EMILY. Tonight.

HARRY. It's not ready.

EMILY. Harry, do not try me.

HARRY. I'm saying

EMILY. And I'm saying I'm not going to argue with you about this. We need a signature dish, since you won't make the scallops.

HARRY. I never said I wouldn't

EMILY. Oh my god you have absolutely refused a dozen times already.

HARRY. I just said that it is impossible to rely on the ingredients and until I can guarantee

EMILY. Harry I am not going to argue with you about this situation with the scallops which is why I have been begging you

HARRY. *(Overlap.)* If I can't get enough scallops to feed the hoards who are now descending on our little enterprise that is hardly my fault, it doesn't make any sense to feed them scallops they are not going to like. You keep acting like I've taken some crazy irrational position here.

EMILY. I know I know I know. I get it. I've heard you. No more scallops. Never again.

(She smiles at him, kisses him quickly.)

HARRY. I never said never.

EMILY. Harry. I'm not talking about scallops right now. I'm talking to you about salmon. This salmon is sublime.

HARRY. Oh, thanks.

EMILY. What is this sauce? It's unbelievable.

HARRY. That's a chutney.

EMILY. Chutney, fantastic. So it's seared salmon with a Bengali chutney.

(She looks for something to write with.)

HARRY. "Bengali"?

EMILY. If you don't like Bengali, give me a better word.

HARRY. Onion?

EMILY. Bengali onion chutney.

HARRY. Bengali is bullshit.

EMILY. And fresh spring asparagus.

(She is writing.)

HARRY. That's redundant.

EMILY. It's not redundant.

HARRY. Asparagus is a spring vegetable.

EMILY. Which is why / it's important to note that we are serving spring asparagus because it acknowledges how particular you are about ingredients. "Locally sourced asparagus" is better.

HARRY. "Locally sourced"?

EMILY. Okay if you don't like

HARRY. "Locally sourced" is something you'd read in a newspaper article, it's not

EMILY. We're on the same side here, Harry. Let's remember that. We both love food, we love your food, your amazing food is why I am here in the first place.

(*She kisses him again.*)

HARRY. I didn't make it for them. I made it for you.

EMILY. (*Mock frustration.*) Harry!

HARRY. What?

EMILY. We're in a kitchen in your restaurant and we need a new signature dish! Of course you made it for them! Now talk to me about your process, what is it that you do to these asparagus spears that gets them to taste like this because honestly no one else out there really can do it. Whatever you are doing is specific and unique and the ingredients are impeccable, so that's what I was

HARRY. (*Shrugging this off now.*) Seared asparagus.

EMILY. "Seared"?

HARRY. They're just seared, in a pan. Olive oil, salt and pepper.

EMILY. "Stovetop seared," then it's seared salmon with a Bengali onion chutney, stovetop-seared asparagus, that's redundant.

HARRY. It's not redundant.

EMILY. Harry you cook, and I'll write.

HARRY. Yeah but you're not using the word right. "Fresh spring" is redundant, "seared" twice is repetitive.

EMILY. What we're trying to do is get the sound of the food to lure the customer into thinking about the taste of the food. So I'm glad that you are interested in this, it really is part of the creative process, obviously. I'm really glad to have engaged in this aspect of the work. Let's just, let's keep talking about the food itself and maybe something else will appear, some idea about the food or the ingredients.

　　　　(A beat.)

HARRY. Well, it's wild salmon.

EMILY. Okay. Okay! Okay. Wild salmon with a Bengali Onion Chutney and fresh spring asparagus.

HARRY. Now there's no searing at all?

EMILY. Harry. We don't have to do this.

HARRY. No, I get it. I totally get it.

　　　　(But he knows the score now. **EMILY** *takes it in and doubles back.)*

EMILY. I mean it.

　　　　(She looks around, making sure she's not heard.)

Turning this place around is not necessarily the best idea I've ever had.

HARRY. Meaning?

EMILY. There's a shortage of chefs out there. I know four places off the top of my head you could walk into tomorrow. Bigger. More resources. And without someone like me breathing down your neck to do things different than the way you want.

HARRY. This is my place.

EMILY. It's Mike's place.

HARRY. We started it together.

EMILY. You can start all over again. I could have a new set of investors out here this weekend, if you'd rather do it that way.

HARRY. Walk out on Mike.

EMILY. Mike's a big boy; he can take care of himself.

HARRY. He'd lose all his money. He'd go bankrupt.

EMILY. It's the restaurant business. It happens all the time.

HARRY. Rodney would have to find another job.

EMILY. There's a shortage of waiters out there as well. He'll be fine.

HARRY. I see.

(He is floored.)

EMILY. Just don't go questioning my loyalty, Harry.

HARRY. I won't.

EMILY. Good.

HARRY. Because I don't think you know what the word "loyalty" means.

(He goes back to the stove. She considers this, shrugs it off.)

EMILY. Maybe we should get back to work.

HARRY. That's a stellar idea.

EMILY. "Seared wild salmon with a Bengali onion chutney and fresh spring asparagus."

(She looks at him. He thinks.)

HARRY. It sounds okay.

EMILY. Great. Great. This is an absolutely beautiful dish, Harry. Thrilling, even. It's terrific to see you working at such a creative peak. It's a crowded marketplace out there and people are looking for something utterly original so it's wonderful to be able to talk about your authentic and restless approach to meals which are so classical in origin.

HARRY. Wow. That shit just comes right out of you, you don't even have to barely pause.

EMILY. We all have our gifts. This is going on the menu, whether you think it's ready or not.

HARRY. The problem is

EMILY. There's no problem.

HARRY. That's wild salmon.

*(Pause. **EMILY** looks at him.)*

EMILY. Wild salmon with a Bengali onion chutney.

HARRY. The Bengali part is bullshit.

EMILY. I don't care.

HARRY. It's wild salmon.

EMILY. Yes, wild salmon, I wrote down –

(She hears what she has just said, and it pisses her off. She takes a breath.)

It's not that hard to get.

HARRY. It's pretty hard to get.

EMILY. How much of it do we have?

HARRY. Four –

EMILY. You only have

HARRY. Four, maybe five servings

EMILY. You only have enough salmon to make four

HARRY. Look. I've been here all night. You asked me

EMILY. I did not ask you

HARRY. You said

EMILY. *(Angry now.)* I said that if you were not willing to put the scallops on the menu that it would be terrific if you could come up with another dish that could take its place as a signature dish, something that people would come here knowing that it was The Thing to order here.

HARRY. You said

EMILY. Something we can put on the menu!

HARRY. You said salmon

EMILY. Something we can put on the menu every night. Salmon counts. People like salmon.

> *(A beat.)*

This doesn't have to be wild salmon.

HARRY. I don't know about "have to be." It just is what it is. It's wild salmon.

EMILY. It could be regular salmon.

HARRY. "Regular," you mean like "farmed" salmon?

EMILY. I'm not playing this game with you, Harry.

HARRY. What game?

EMILY. Mike maybe enjoys it but I don't.

HARRY. I'm not playing anything.

EMILY. We're putting this on the menu.

HARRY. I only have enough wild salmon

EMILY. I heard you the first time. You are right, wild salmon is if anything more difficult to find than the freshest deep water scallops handpicked off the ocean floor by the Little Mermaid herself.

HARRY. Well now I don't know what you're talking about.

EMILY. Tomorrow I am going to go out and get you the best farmed salmon I can find. And you are going to practice making this DELICIOUS seared salmon with Bengali Onion CHUTNEY using farmed salmon. And then we will see how we like that. For now, it will not go on the menu. Because we don't have enough of it, to serve.

HARRY. Okay.

EMILY. What would you like to put on the menu for this evening, Harry?

HARRY. I leave it up to you, Emily.

EMILY. Well, I'm just going to go out front and have a glass, maybe a lovely glass of Pinot, or two, and I'm going to think about what might be a fun menu for tonight. That's what I'm going to do, then.

*(She goes, passing **MIKE** who is entering.)*

We're calling it seared salmon with asparagus I don't give a shit about how shitty it sounds.

*(She is gone. **MIKE** looks at **HARRY**.)*

MIKE. What'd you do to her?

HARRY. I didn't do anything!

MIKE. Honest to god Harry, you promised that you would make this work.

HARRY. I am making it work! She asked for something to put on the menu to replace the scallops.

MIKE. Why are we replacing the scallops? Everybody loved the scallops, they ask for them every night, why can't you just make the fucking scallops?

HARRY. Look I'm not going back to why. She wanted some more seafood choices so that's what I gave her and now she's all pissed off, I don't know why. I did what she asked me to do and now she's pissed.

(**MIKE** *sees the salmon on the counter.*)

MIKE. This is the new dish?

HARRY. Seared wild salmon with Bengali onion chutney.

(**MIKE** *looks at him.*)

MIKE. You are a fucking asshole.

HARRY. Why? Why does that make me an asshole?

MIKE. She asked you for a new seafood dish to put on the menu because you're such a fucking snob about scallops and the only thing harder to find than a decent scallop is wild fucking salmon.

HARRY. I stayed here all night cooking, coming up with something new and hopefully delicious

MIKE. (*Checking off his fingers.*) Tilapia. Shrimp. Halibut. Branzino.

HARRY. And all I get, from you and her both is

MIKE. All of which are popular, sustainable seafood. Flounder. Sole. There are a million – not to mention chicken, or steak!

HARRY. She didn't want chicken or steak or anything vegan, there were a lot of restrictions on what I was allowed to try for my new "signature dish."

MIKE. You hate vegan! If someone told you to cook something vegan you'd go to the mats for a week destroying the whole idea of veganism.

HARRY. Vegans are idiots.

MIKE. You were asked to come up with a beautiful recipe that she could promote. That we could put on the menu consistently.

HARRY. Not consistently. Always. Always.

MIKE. Yes, always. We need a few things on the menu that we always have! This is common sense! This is –

> (*A beat.*)

It's not an outrage to ask for this. It's common sense.

> (*He stops, shakes his head.* **HARRY** *is unapologetic.*)

HARRY. Food is not common sense. It doesn't work that way.

MIKE. Harry.

HARRY. I said yes to the whole idea of "Emily" because you were right, you put a lot of yourself into this place and so did I but the financial burden I had not fully considered, and so I agreed to this arrangement, with Emily, and I have been trying.

MIKE. This isn't trying! Building a great recipe around an ingredient which is –

HARRY. Wild salmon is a great ingredient; done properly it can be the soul of a great meal.

MIKE. It is seasonal. It is expensive. It is hard to source.

HARRY. You haven't even tasted it!

MIKE. I'm not going to taste it.

HARRY. Oh that's mature.

MIKE. Mature? Did you just

HARRY. You're not going to even taste it?

MIKE. Would you consider making it with farmed salmon?

HARRY. Whether or not I would

MIKE. Would you?

HARRY. Let me finish.

MIKE. Answer the question.

HARRY. You're literally not going to even taste it. If I say no. It has to be wild salmon. That would stop you from tasting it.

(They stare at each other for a long moment.)

MIKE. Are you saying that?

HARRY. You know what? You guys have a lot of rules about what makes a great menu and you both talk to me like I'm an idiot or an insane person. You talk like I don't know how to build a menu after I've been doing it for YEARS. First I did it for people who I didn't want to work for, and then I did it for myself. For years. People love my menus, they love the way I run a restaurant –

MIKE. The way "we" run a restaurant.

HARRY. Okay, WE run the restaurant, and I make the menu. Because I'm the fucking chef. And people come here to eat MY food and I don't need anyone telling me what to cook or how to cook. That is not the deal. Fuck you. I would say fuck you both but I've already said it to her so the person I need to say fuck you to right now is, you, Mike.

(They stare at each other.)

MIKE. You want me to taste it.

HARRY. I don't give a shit if you taste it.

MIKE. If you don't give a shit, then I'm not going to taste it.

HARRY. Oh stop it you are too.

MIKE. You're a complete child.

HARRY. You want to go back to this? Fuck you. I'm not a child. I'm the person who's been holding this restaurant together, yes you run the place but I am the BEATING HEART of the operation, I know who I am and what I do, and there's nothing wrong with my character. You want the world to be different? You don't like the deal we made two and a half years ago and you want to change things? I gave you that against all of my better impulses, you already got me agreeing to that bullshit even though I don't agree with any of it. But when you tell me to be someone I'm not? I'm not going to do that for you.

MIKE. This isn't about your essential identity! It's about a fucking piece of salmon!

HARRY. You think that because you're you, and I'm me.

MIKE. Why is this so impossible? Even a simple discussion

HARRY. You think this discussion is simple?

MIKE. I think I would love it if every time someone came up with an idea it didn't turn into eight days of wrangling.

HARRY. If it was a decent idea it wouldn't.

> (*A pause.*)

MIKE. It's a piece of fish, Harry.

HARRY. That's what I'm saying.

> (*Another pause.* **MIKE** *reaches for the plate. He takes a bite. There is a pause, while he eats it.*)

MIKE. Okay. That is delicious.

HARRY. Thank you.

MIKE. It's a little greasy. Not the salmon. The chutney.

HARRY. (*Surprised.*) The chutney?

(He reaches over and spears a forkful himself.)

MIKE. What is...there's something, what is the thing in the chutney that is making it

HARRY. I put a little of the oil from the anchovies. Wild salmon gets a little

MIKE. *(Figuring it out.)* That's what it is. It's just

HARRY. It's just a hint, in case. I don't think it's greasy.

MIKE. It comes at the palate, at the end of the bite in a way that, it's decadent for sure. If that's what you're going for, okay, but...

HARRY. No, I see I see. I get it.

> *(***MIKE*** has another bite. ***HARRY*** does too. They eat for a moment. ***RODNEY*** enters from the back, watches them eat.)*

RODNEY. What are you eating?

HARRY. Just some salmon.

MIKE. You could make it with farmed salmon.

HARRY. Listen.

MIKE. Yes the wild salmon stands up to the chutney.

RODNEY. Can I?

> *(They push the plate over for ***RODNEY*** to taste. He gets himself a fork.)*

MIKE. I'm just saying it won't take anything away. If you just use the anchovy, the fattier fish will hold the flavor without needing the extra oil.

RODNEY. Yeah, this is good.

HARRY. "Good"?

RODNEY. The wild salmon dries out so fast. Plus I think it's kind of loud.

HARRY. "Loud"?

RODNEY. Like, loud in your mouth. You'd be better off with farmed. Which they're saying is okay to cook with now.

HARRY. If you're okay with cooking with ingredients that are "okay."

RODNEY. No seriously, they addressed the stuff people were concerned about. It's safe and delicious and you get your omega threes. Salmon makes people happy. I love salmon. This is terrific, I just think it would taste better with farmed salmon. When you sear it up, you get that nice crusty bit at the end, I love that part.

> (*He continues to eat the food. At one point he even licks his fingers.* **HARRY** *sighs, goes to the door, and grabs his jacket.*)

MIKE. Where are you going?

HARRY. I'm going to the Key Food to buy some farmed salmon!

> (**HARRY** *is gone.* **MIKE** *watches* **RODNEY** *eat.*)

MIKE. How come he listens to you but he won't listen to me.

RODNEY. I'm pure.

MIKE. You're pure?

RODNEY. Yeah, I got no agenda.

MIKE. I don't have an agenda.

RODNEY. You totally have an agenda. Your agenda is money.

MIKE. My agenda is the success of this restaurant! We've been trapped in this restaurant for two and a half years, my "agenda" is to make some money and THEN we're free. Then we can do whatever we want.

RODNEY. Yeah I've heard that before. Dudes I grew up with, dealing coke on street corners all talking about what's going to happen when they got enough money. They all ended up in jail. Not just the Black guys, the white guys too.

(**MIKE** *shakes his head, pissed.*)

MIKE. What did you say?

RODNEY. I'm just talking.

MIKE. You walk around here in a new leather jacket and then you sneer at me about making money.

RODNEY. I was just talking.

MIKE. *(Pissed now.)* I'm not going to jail and I'm not a coke dealer. I'm a normal human being, I have normal human feelings and dreams and I work hard and I'm not a completely fucked-up self-destructive genius. That doesn't make me a a cokehead or the head of fucking Deutsche Bank. I'm running a restaurant.

RODNEY. I didn't mean that.

(**MIKE** *looks in the fridge.*)

MIKE. And of course he hasn't even started this week's prep.

RODNEY. He's got his hands full with that Emily.

MIKE. Meaning what?

RODNEY. What? We all got our hands full with Emily.

(*He starts working, washing carrots.* **MIKE** *sits in silence for a long moment, watching him.*)

MIKE. Okay I have to tell you something. And you can't tell Harry.

RODNEY. *(Startled.)* Oh. You know, I don't...

MIKE. We have a critic coming in three days.

RODNEY. We got a critic coming?

> *(He stops what he's doing, looks at* **MIKE**. **MIKE** *nods.)*

MIKE. Emily has been working on something. Arranging a review.

RODNEY. Is that what you do with reviews now? You arrange them?

MIKE. You know as well as I do they're not easy to get.

RODNEY. We had some bullshit nobody just walk in off the street.

MIKE. That was a puff piece. That was nothing.

RODNEY. We're bursting at the seams!

MIKE. That's right we are and people have noticed and now we're getting reviewed.

RODNEY. But Harry doesn't know about it.

MIKE. He will know about it. Of course Harry is going to know about it.

RODNEY. But he doesn't yet.

MIKE. No, not yet.

RODNEY. When are you going to tell him?

MIKE. Emily is going to present it to him.

RODNEY. Emily?

MIKE. She thought it would be better coming from her.

RODNEY. How come?

MIKE. This is a complicated situation. Harry is potentially going to be a little reactive. So we're going to let Emily handle it.

RODNEY. I don't know, Mike. She's a tricky customer. You know she and Harry already... Well, you know.

MIKE. You've got to be kidding me.

RODNEY. You're the one who brought her in!

MIKE. Oh my god.

> (**MIKE**'s *mind is racing while he adds that element into this mess, and his temper is rising again.*)

RODNEY. So, you really want me to not tell Harry.

MIKE. Is that a problem?

RODNEY. You know, it is, kind of.

MIKE. Oh my god I am so tired of arguing about absolutely everything with absolutely everybody.

RODNEY. Yeah, but you just told me to lie to Harry.

MIKE. I'm not telling you to lie!

RODNEY. Oh, no, huh.

MIKE. It's not your place to share the information. You know what? It's not your place to judge this either. If you have a problem with me or Emily or the way any of this is being handled, you can leave.

RODNEY. Whoa, what?

MIKE. You heard me. You tell Harry anything about this critic showing up, and I'll fire you.

RODNEY. You can't fire me.

MIKE. Trust me. I can, and I will.

> (*Lights shift.*)

Scene Three

*(Night. **MIKE** at the counter with his laptop.
HARRY is cleaning, **RODNEY** enters, counting
his money.)*

RODNEY. That six top, all those chicks, somebody's
birthday party? Left a bullshit tip.

MIKE. How much did they leave?

RODNEY. Thirty-two bucks.

HARRY. What'd they have?

(He is looking through the receipts.)

RODNEY. Salmon, gnocchi, salads, four bottles of Prosecco

HARRY. They did, they stiffed you.

RODNEY. Sometimes you're up, sometimes you're down.

HARRY. *(Laughing.)* What is that, the Tao Te Ching?

RODNEY. That's me, working in a restaurant.

*(He pockets his dough. **EMILY** enters, with the
ledger. **RODNEY** watches her, wary.)*

EMILY. Harry, leave that alone. I told you, we have a cleaning
crew coming in the morning, they'll take care of it.

HARRY. A cleaning crew. How much is that going to cost us?

EMILY. It's not going to cost you anything; it's coming out
of your profits. Which have doubled, as I'm sure you
know. Now, both of you, out of here. Mike and I will
close up.

HARRY. Hang on.

EMILY. Harry for once can you not argue about something?
You cooked like a titan tonight. Everything was
impeccable as usual and you've earned the rest of the
night off. Mike?

MIKE. The cleaning crew is coming whether you want them or not. They've already been paid for.

HARRY. I just –

EMILY. Good night!

RODNEY. You don't have to tell me four times.

HARRY. Guess I'll go home and see what's on my Netflix queue.

RODNEY. Yeah, when was the last time you did that?

HARRY. Back in 1997. Back when Netflix still had queues.

> (**RODNEY** *goes.* **HARRY** *shrugs, grabs his coat and follows him. He looks back at* **MIKE** *and* **EMILY**. **EMILY** *smiles and waves, while* **MIKE** *continues to work.* **HARRY** *goes.* **EMILY** *thinks for a moment.)*
>
> (*She reaches for a half-empty bottle of red, glances at the label, starts to pour.)*

EMILY. What's up with you?

MIKE. Nothing is "up" with me.

EMILY. Mike, it is my job to know when my client is not happy.

MIKE. Are you sleeping with Harry?

EMILY. Not at the moment, no.

MIKE. But you did. You slept with him.

EMILY. I'm not suing anyone for sexual harassment if that's what you're asking.

MIKE. I can't believe this.

EMILY. It's a restaurant. Things happen. Things get heated and then they get more heated.

MIKE. I'm aware of how restaurants work.

EMILY. I didn't think we needed to get your permission.

MIKE. Is it an ongoing situation?

EMILY. You want details?

MIKE. *(Blunt.)* Yeah. I do.

EMILY. *(Brushing this aside.)* It is not ongoing. It was a few nights.

MIKE. Was that strategic?

EMILY. Oh my god. What are you accusing me of?

MIKE. I'm not accusing you of anything. I'm just...

EMILY. You're tired. We all are. Which is how Harry and I ended up in the sack together. I don't think it's anything you need to worry about.

(*She goes back to work.*)

MIKE. Why haven't you told him we're being reviewed?

EMILY. Like I told you, this critic is a friend and he wanted to come in under the radar.

MIKE. You didn't say that meant don't tell Harry at all.

EMILY. It doesn't mean that. It just means that I would prefer to be the one to tell him.

MIKE. But you haven't.

EMILY. I'm going to tell him! But you know as well as I do it's never clear.

MIKE. Emily, you are as clear as a rock that someone is bashing your head with.

(*She turns and look at him, chilly.*)

I shouldn't have said that. I don't even know what that means.

EMILY. No, it's very flattering.

MIKE. I just don't understand why Harry hasn't been told yet!

EMILY. Harry hasn't been told yet because he doesn't need to know yet.

MIKE. He does need to know, if a critic is about to show up and expect the royal treatment –

EMILY. *(Overlap.)* He can't handle the critics, why should he be put into a position where he's just going to sabotage himself yet again.

MIKE. Harry is a consummate professional and you know it.

EMILY. *(Overlap.)* Oh my god the last time someone showed up and said something nice about his cooking, he refused to make the same dish ever again!

MIKE. I told Rodney.

EMILY. You told Rodney...

MIKE. There are only four people who work here. He needs to know.

EMILY. You told Rodney that we may be –

MIKE. Not may be, you told me definitely.

EMILY. But definitely only ever means maybe.

MIKE. That's not what you said.

EMILY. I told you

MIKE. The point is I told him. And he raised the question of why Harry hasn't been told yet. And I think he's right.

EMILY. He cannot tell him.

MIKE. He's not going to tell him.

EMILY. He said that. You were clear about that. He agreed to that?

MIKE. Yes. I threatened him. I threatened to fire him if he didn't.

> (**EMILY** *is coolly impressed with that bit of news.*)

EMILY. Good.

MIKE. My point is, Emily, that the guy – the guy is going to show up! You can say now that maybe he's not going to show up? But when he shows up, you can't just spring that on Harry.

EMILY. Oh, please. If telling Harry about it would get us something, I would tell him. Here, let's phrase this another way. If I do give Harry a heads up, what do you think will happen?

> (**MIKE** *is sad, silenced.*)

MIKE. You have to tell him. You have to let him go through whatever his fucked up process is. You have to tell him.

EMILY. *(Firm.)* Do not make the mistake of thinking that I don't know how to handle a temperamental chef. It's not like I've never encountered this guy before. They all think they're so special. Every reasonably talented guy out there has been told that he's a fucking genius at some point in his life and let me tell you they all believe it and they've been believing it since they were four which is frankly when they stopped developing psychologically. And that's not to say that Harry isn't actually special; clearly I think he is, or I wouldn't be here. But being special and knowing that you're special and also having an attitude about the fact that you're so special – that ultimately makes you a little less special, doesn't it? I mean, maybe "special" doesn't mean you're an "artist," maybe it just means you're an asshole with some talent. And if that's all you are? Then self-destructive bullshit really will bring you down.

MIKE. Wow, I bet you were a lot of fun in the sack.

EMILY. I've never had any complaints.

MIKE. You know, you and I – we don't actually have anything in writing.

EMILY. Meaning what?

MIKE. Meaning maybe we should walk away from this.

EMILY. Maybe we should. There are a million restaurants out there that could use me. And then you'll have nothing. I'm not here by accident, Mike. You guys were going down. Critics are always a risk. But I've looked at your books, remember? You are out of wiggle room. This works, or it doesn't.

MIKE. This is so fucked.

EMILY. It's not fucked. It's difficult. Life is difficult sometimes.

> (**MIKE** *thinks about this, sighs. He heads out, stops and looks at the kitchen. Then, deliberate, he turns back to* **EMILY**.)

MIKE. Every night I go to bed wishing I could cook like that.

> *(He goes.)*

> *(Blackout.)*

Scene Four

(Three days later. **HARRY** *takes a plate of salmon out of the oven.* **RODNEY** *watches him.* **HARRY** *looks at it, considers something, starts to chop some onions. It's dazzling.)*

RODNEY. So which is the one you picked?

*(***EMILY*** *enters. They don't see her at first.)*

HARRY. The Kikuichi.

RODNEY. How come you picked that one?

HARRY. I like the way it feels. It grows out of your arm right. It's got strength. You almost don't even have to do anything, it floats. Sort of like a bird wing. It's subtle.

(He shows **RODNEY**, *who watches.)*

EMILY. Rodney, can you write that down?

RODNEY. Oh. You want me to –

EMILY. It's beautiful. Perfect. You're a poet, Harry.

HARRY. Gee, thanks, Emily. I live for your praise, as you know.

EMILY. I do know that, Harry.

(She hands **HARRY** *a piece of paper, then goes to* **RODNEY**.)*

"It's like a bird wing."

RODNEY. I got it.

HARRY. What's this.

EMILY. It's the menu.

HARRY. We don't print menus.

EMILY. There's no law against it.

HARRY. There's no law that says you have to do it, either.

EMILY. Well, in the absence of direction from the gods of food, I have decided we should give it a whirl. Just see how it goes for a couple of days. Okay?

HARRY. We never have menus. Our people don't want them.

EMILY. Your people do want them, they ask for them all the time.

HARRY. You show them the board.

EMILY. Harry, menus are easy. You type them up on a laptop, you pick a cute little font, and then take it to the copy place across the street, they cost ten dollars to print out and look how nice they look.

HARRY. And now I have to cook this stuff?

EMILY. You told me that was tonight's menu.

HARRY. What if I change my mind.

EMILY. Then you say we ran out or there's a new special, you do it all the time.

HARRY. Which is why we don't need menus.

EMILY. *(Snapping finally.)* People like menus. I'm not apologizing for this.

> *(***RODNEY*** *hands her the page he was writing on.)*

Thank you, Rodney. I'm sure Kikuichi will really appreciate your endorsement, Harry.

HARRY. I didn't say –

EMILY. You did, and I didn't even make you write it down! Kikuichi doesn't give those things away just to be nice, you have to write an endorsement.

RODNEY. *(Genuinely pleased.)* Look at this. We got menus. Got your salmon on here.

HARRY. I'm aware. There's six hundred pieces of farmed salmon in the fridge, waiting obediently to be cooked, plated and served.

RODNEY. Come on.

EMILY. Not six hundred!

HARRY. A lot.

(**RODNEY** *is looking into the fridge, laughs.*)

EMILY. What's Mike doing?

RODNEY. He's on the phone with some guy from the dishware place.

HARRY. He's talking to José?

EMILY. We're using a new service.

HARRY. Why?

EMILY. José wasn't sure he could handle the higher volume.

HARRY. *(Overlap.)* We've been using José for two years.

EMILY. Yes, and he was always late.

HARRY. Aw come on! I've been going along with all of this and I don't like it but I did not agree / that you could fire people.

EMILY. *(Overlap, louder.)* José was very clear about what he can and can't do right now he is very busy and cannot handle the extra volume.

HARRY. Well I don't agree to that.

EMILY. It doesn't matter if you agree. If Mike agrees and I agree we outvote you, Harry.

HARRY. "Outvote"? Did you just say "outvote"?

EMILY. José said

HARRY. You don't get a vote, Emily. You are a consultant as I recall.

RODNEY. You want me to go get Mike?

EMILY. No.

HARRY. Yes.

EMILY. I would really love it if you could go give Mike a hand in the dining room for a moment, Rodney. I'll let you know when we need him.

> (**RODNEY** *goes. There is a tense moment from* **EMILY**. **HARRY**, *on the other hand, is reasonably pleased with himself.*)

Okay. Okay, Harry. Here's the thing.

HARRY. Yes?

EMILY. You don't hate money. You love it. You love everyone telling you how delicious your food is. You love the applause, and the excitement. You even love me.

HARRY. I don't love you, Emily.

EMILY. You love something about me.

HARRY. I don't.

EMILY. We don't have to get stuck on that. Let's talk about this situation with *New York Magazine*.

HARRY. The guy liked my scallops. I've heard.

EMILY. And then you refused to cook them again. He gave you guys a nice little bump of attention, and then you tried to throw that down the drain.

HARRY. I did no such thing.

EMILY. No you didn't because I wouldn't let you.

HARRY. Perhaps now would be a good time to remind you that you are not the boss of me, Emily.

EMILY. Perhaps now would be a good time to remind you that you are not the boss of yourself, Harry. You're so mired in self-aggrandizement and illusion you were on the brink of destroying everything you love when I showed up.

HARRY. Because I was tired of cooking scallops?

EMILY. You are utterly self-destructive, and that's how deluded you are, you haven't even noticed.

HARRY. I'm deluded now?

EMILY. You are, but I am not. There is a critic coming tonight.

HARRY. Really.

EMILY. I'm not going to tell you his name or who he writes for. I will say, he's not insignificant.

HARRY. He's NOT insignificant.

EMILY. If he likes your food, he can make you a destination. Would you like to be a destination, Harry?

HARRY. As opposed to a human being?

EMILY. That's right.

HARRY. Let's back up before I answer that. This nameless critic is coming tonight?

EMILY. Yes. Tonight.

HARRY. And you're not going to tell me his name.

EMILY. No I'm not.

HARRY. Is it Voldemort?

EMILY. Which would be why I'm not telling you his name.

HARRY. What time is he coming?

EMILY. I don't know.

HARRY. You don't know?

EMILY. He is very generously squeezing us in. He wasn't sure when. But he is coming.

HARRY. And nobody thought that maybe I needed to know about that?

EMILY. Mike didn't want to worry you.

HARRY. Mike didn't want to WORRY me?

EMILY. No, he didn't. He felt in fact like there were too many changes happening too fast, and that stressing you out would be detrimental.

HARRY. Mike told you not to tell me.

EMILY. It was not a decision anyone made lightly. We weren't sure if it was happening but now it is. And it's major.

HARRY. *(Pissed.)* It's the *Times*?

EMILY. I'm not saying it's the *Times*. I'm not saying it's not the *Times*. It is someone who can make or break you.

HARRY. I don't need to be made, or broken, Emily.

>   (**RODNEY** *comes in. He is spooked.*)

What?

RODNEY. Nothing. Nothing. There's a couple people out there. They want the wilted spinach salad with the warm bacon dressing and the gnocchi and the salmon and the um veal and they also wanted to know if they could get the scallops.

HARRY. The scallops aren't on the menu.

RODNEY. They asked me to ask you.

>   (**MIKE** *enters.* **EMILY** *looks at him, turns and heads out into the dining room.*)

EMILY. Excuse me.

>   (*She is gone. There is a pause.* **HARRY** *shakes his head.*)

HARRY. What?

MIKE. Just a table walked in.

HARRY. Little early for that, isn't it? We don't officially open for ten minutes.

MIKE. They asked if I'd make an exception for them.

HARRY. And why would we do that?

MIKE. Just to be nice.

(**HARRY** *shakes his head, pissed.*)

HARRY. Who is it?

MIKE. It doesn't matter who it is.

HARRY. Obviously it matters more than anything else in the universe. Whoever it is, we're about to sell our souls in every way possible, in order to make them happy.

MIKE. This is a good thing, Harry.

HARRY. This is bullshit.

MIKE. This is everything we wanted.

HARRY. You lied to me.

MIKE. I never lied to you.

HARRY. That – critic – is out there –

MIKE. That critic is out there yes because he has heard that

HARRY. What has he heard and who has he heard it from

MIKE. He's heard you're good, Harry. He's heard you're great!

HARRY. Oh is that what he's heard?

MIKE. *(Startled.)* Yes.

(**HARRY** *is pissed, worried.* **MIKE** *is taken aback.*)

What are you worried about?

HARRY. I'm worried that you didn't tell me. That's why I'm worried. If this critic is so important, why didn't you tell me?

MIKE. We're telling you now.

HARRY. I'm not ready.

MIKE. You're always ready, what are you talking about.

HARRY. You can't do this to me, Mike. You seriously can't – all this stuff we've been doing, I don't like it but I do it. But you got to tell me, you have to.

MIKE. We couldn't tell you, you argue about everything.

HARRY. I argue because

MIKE. You argue because you like to argue

HARRY. I argue because things have to be a certain way for me to do what I do, you can't just

MIKE. You say that, Harry, but then you always manage to pull it off.

HARRY. Not this. You can't just

MIKE. You've cooked everything on that order a hundred times. The wilted spinach salad, even I can do that.

HARRY. You can't do it, you always put too much balsamic on the plate.

MIKE. You do it then. Do it.

> (**EMILY** *reenters, all business. There is an air of seriousness to this that is unmistakable.*)

EMILY. There's another party at the four top in the window. Rodney, could you go take their drink orders?

RODNEY. Sure.

> (*He goes.*)

MIKE. Did you take care of…?

EMILY. Yes I did. I started them with a couple of glasses of Prosecco, they should be fine for a few minutes. Harry are you with us? They want to split the spinach salad.

MIKE. Do they want to split the gnocchi?

EMILY. They didn't say anything about it so we'll just serve it on a single plate. You don't want to pander. Harry, you're going to have to suck it up and do those scallops.

HARRY. They're not on the menu.

EMILY. They've asked for you to make them. I told them we'd check.

HARRY. I thought you didn't want to pander.

EMILY. It's a fluid position. Could we get you moving on that salad? It's a little weird that he's here so early, usually they only do that when they have someplace else to be so he's going to be acutely aware of how quickly things come out of the kitchen. We don't want to give him anything to carp on.

> (**HARRY** goes to the refrigerator, opens it. **EMILY** is quickly impatient.)

What is the problem, Harry?

> (She sets up the plating for the wilted spinach salad.)

HARRY. I want to see him.

> (**MIKE** and **EMILY** step in front of the door.)

EMILY. You don't want to see him. More importantly he doesn't want to be seen. This is important to some critics, the myth of invisibility.

HARRY. People are not invisible.

MIKE. You won't recognize him anyway. He's nobody you know.

HARRY. Then why do I care what he thinks about my food?

EMILY. You don't care what he thinks about your food. You are just going to cook a delicious meal for him, and leave the caring to us.

HARRY. Okay. Okay.

> (**HARRY** *looks at them both. He picks up his knife. He looks around.*)

MIKE. What? What are you looking for ?

HARRY. Bacon.

> (**EMILY** *finds the bacon.*)

EMILY. (*Sharp.*) What is the matter, Harry? Is this a particularly difficult salad to make?

HARRY. No. No! I'm just, just give me a minute.

EMILY. Mike, maybe you could put some water on for the gnocchi.

> (**MIKE** *moves toward the sink.*)

HARRY. I can take care of boiling water, Mike.

> (**HARRY** *goes to the sink, grabs a pot along the way, starts to fill it with water. But he is sweating. He turns the water off, looks at the full pot.*)

EMILY. What is the problem, Harry?

> (**EMILY** *grabs the pot of water from him, and puts it on another burner.* **HARRY** *lets her.* **RODNEY** *enters.*)

RODNEY. You need me to take those salads out?

HARRY. Just give me a minute!

> (*He snarls it. But there's something different in all this.* **RODNEY** *looks at him, at the others, startled.*)

RODNEY. I can plate those salads.

HARRY. Back off. I mean it, back off.

> *(He picks up his new knife, looks at it. He is actually confused.)*

EMILY. Harry –

HARRY. *(To* **RODNEY**.*)* You knew he was coming, too.

RODNEY. Mike told me.

HARRY. So why didn't you tell me?

RODNEY. He told me not to.

EMILY. Rodney, would you please start those salads.

HARRY. You back off, Emily. This is still my kitchen.

MIKE. No one said it wasn't. Look, we're all nervous, maybe this wasn't handled right, but we are here now and we are not going to blow this.

> *(He puts his hand on* **HARRY***'s shoulder.* **HARRY** *looks at him, confused.)*

HARRY. It doesn't feel right to me. I mean it. It feels crazy.

MIKE. It's not. We worked hard for a long time. I know this last part has been rough. But you have to see it as a whole thing. I want my life back. And it's been gone for a long time. Longer than you know. We got to take this to the next level, or we'll lose all of it. We'll lose each other.

HARRY. Why didn't you just tell me?

MIKE. You're not the easiest guy to explain things to.

HARRY. Yeah, but...

MIKE. Harry, all you got to do is cook. You love to cook. Do it because you love it.

(**EMILY** *is about to say something.* **MIKE** *holds up his hand. She stays silent. There is a pause.* **HARRY** *moves to the stove, he moves a pan. Looks at the boiling water. Drops bacon into the heated skillet. He takes a breath.*)

HARRY. What'd I do with the onions?

MIKE. They're right here.

HARRY. Rodney, can you grab me one of those salmon filets? It's gonna need to temper.

RODNEY. Got it.

(**RODNEY** *gets the salmon out of the refrigerator.*)

HARRY. Someone go find out what kind of clock they're on. Why'd they show up this early, do they need to make it back to midtown for something?

EMILY. I'll ask.

HARRY. Find out specifically what time. I don't want to throw everything at them at once if I don't have to.

HARRY. What's on the other ticket?

RODNEY. What other ticket?

HARRY. *(Impatient.)* The four top in the window.

RODNEY. Oh.

HARRY. Mike.

(**MIKE** *goes.* **HARRY** *continues to cook.* **RODNEY** *helps him, silently holding out the plates for the wilted spinach salad.*)

RODNEY. I didn't mean to.

HARRY. We're not going to talk about it.

RODNEY. I was going to tell you, Harry, honestly, but it wasn't my place. And Mike was worked up. He said he would fire me if I told you.

HARRY. *(Looks at him, then.)* We'll talk about it later.

RODNEY. I know it was fucked up.

> *(For a moment, the two* **MEN** *cook together. Having finished the salad,* **HARRY** *drizzles dressing on the salad plates, hands them to* **RODNEY**, *who takes them out as* **EMILY** *reenters.)*

EMILY. They're hoping to make an eight o'clock curtain, so they have to be out of here by seven fifteen.

HARRY. Okay. We'll get the gnocchi in the water as soon as they've started on the salads, then have the salmon and the veal ready to go by six thirty. Then if they want dessert there's still time.

EMILY. And the scallops.

HARRY. I got no scallops.

EMILY. No –

HARRY. Emily, you listen to me now. There is a point beyond which no one can go. There are no scallops in this kitchen and I would not cook them even if they were here. But they aren't here, so we don't have to have that conversation. Instead, you can go out there and tell your friends who are in way too big a hurry because they double booked themselves tonight that there are no scallops on the menu and there are no scallops in my restaurant and if they want scallops they can go somewhere else.

EMILY. I'm not going to tell them that.

HARRY. There are no scallops.

EMILY. There are, actually. Mike picked them up.

> *(**MIKE** reenters on this. **HARRY** looks at him.)*

MIKE. *(Awkward.)* Emily thought – she was pulling a lot of favors to get this guy out here. And she was pretty sure he'd want the scallops.

HARRY. You promised him scallops?

EMILY. It wasn't a promise. But in my enthusiasm for your cooking I may have raved about your scallops, Harry, everybody does.

HARRY. I don't do the scallops anymore.

EMILY. You don't but you can.

MIKE. It's okay, Harry.

HARRY. Would you stop talking to me like I'm some sort of irredeemable idiot?

> *(He turns back to the stovetop, moves a few pots around.)*

MIKE. Are you going to –

HARRY. I got this, Mike. I got this.

> *(**RODNEY** reenters, with the order from the other table.)*

RODNEY. Grilled calamari, beet salad, the salmon and – okay don't shoot the messenger, they want to know if they can order the scallops? They heard Emily talking to the other table, maybe we have them tonight, even though they're not on the menu?

> *(A beat.)*

HARRY. Well. How many orders of scallops did you pick up, Mike?

MIKE. I got about three pounds.

HARRY. Three pounds! Wow. Isn't that lucky. That's enough scallops for a whole restaurant full of critics.

MIKE. I was just being careful. I went to the guy you like, up on Flatbush.

HARRY. They any good?

MIKE. They looked good to me, yeah.

> *(Relieved, he goes to the refrigerator.* **RODNEY** *and* **EMILY** *watch as* **MIKE** *reaches in and digs around.)*

HARRY. You hid them pretty good in there, huh?

MIKE. Look. I just didn't know...

HARRY. I get it. I get it.

> *(He takes the scallops from* **MIKE**, *looks at them.)*

EMILY. Where are we at with the gnocchi?

HARRY. Cool your jets, Emily.

EMILY. There isn't time, Harry!

> *(***HARRY*** sniffs the scallops, then finds a dish. He pours the scallops into the dish. He considers them.)*

Oh my god. You're doing this deliberately.

HARRY. They look good.

MIKE. They are good. I told him they were for you. He wanted you to know. They're fresh, they're sweet. He was really confident you'd be happy.

RODNEY. Harry, you want me to...

HARRY. Just give me a second, Rodney.

EMILY. *(An eruption.)* GOD, could someone in this fucking kitchen do some fucking cooking?

> *(***HARRY*** sets the bowl of scallops down. He turns and looks at the stove, the burners going, the scallops waiting. He turns back and looks at the others.)*

HARRY. *(Confused again.)* I can't.

(He holds his hand to his chest. Then he shakes his head.)

I can't.

(He goes out the back door. **EMILY** *flips.)*

EMILY. You CAN'T? Harry where are you going? HARRY. I'm going to kill him. I'm going to fucking kill him.

(To **MIKE**.*)* And then I'm going to kill you. This is your fault. You said you could handle him. You said he wouldn't flip out.

MIKE. I –

EMILY. FUCK YOU.

(Then.)

Harry. HARRY.

(She heads out back, after him. **MIKE** *and* **RODNEY** *look at each other, startled.)*

RODNEY. What happened? What's going on?

MIKE. Fuck him.

(He walks away from the door.)

RODNEY. Don't just stand there. Go get him!

*(**RODNEY** goes and gets the gnocchi and starts cooking.)*

MIKE. FUCK HIM. I don't need him.

RODNEY. Oh yes you do. Get out of the way!

(He shoves **MIKE** *out of the way, starts cooking.)*

You know what this sucks. I could have told you this wouldn't work. You let that psychopath run things what did you think was going to happen?

MIKE. I'm TIRED of the psychopath. He can just learn to behave like a normal human being.

RODNEY. Not Harry. Emily! Emily's the psychopath you moron.

MIKE. Two and a half years. My LIFE. Every penny I own. I'm RUINED. You know that? This will ruin me.

RODNEY. Get out of my way.

> (**RODNEY** *is cooking now, as fast as he can.*
> *He gets a dish, finds a pot with clarified butter*
> *in it, drops a lump into the dish, then goes to*
> *the island, where he picks up Harry's knife.*
> *He looks around and finds Harry's stash of*
> *sage leaves, starts to shred it.*)

MIKE. One dish. I threw my whole life behind the idea that that lunatic should have his own kitchen, and it's too much to make the one fucking dish that might save me from BANKRUPTCY. I'm nothing to him! I'm just the idiot who told him he was an artist that his food was ART and I made it true, I gave him everything he ever wanted and now I have nothing because his fucking pride can't take the fact that he actually has to cook something that he cooks brilliantly anyway, he can do all of these dishes with his eyes closed but the idea that someone might show up and JUDGE him is such a fucking offense he'd rather ruin me. Fuck him. Fuck people. Fuck all of it.

> (**RODNEY** *has been cooking through all of*
> *that. He finishes up the bowl of gnocchi,*
> *sprinkling sage leaves on it, and heads out to*
> *the table.* **MIKE**, *alone, looks around, bereft.*
> **EMILY** *returns, alone.*)

He's not coming back.

EMILY. Apparently not, no. Where's Rodney.

MIKE. He took the gnocchi out...

EMILY. The gnocchi? Who made the gnocchi?

MIKE. He did.

EMILY. How was it? Mike! Did you taste it?

MIKE. No.

>   (**RODNEY** *returns.*)

RODNEY. Where's Harry?

EMILY. You made the gnocchi?

RODNEY. Somebody had to.

>   (*She goes out to the dining room.* **MIKE** *and*
>   **RODNEY**, *alone. After a moment,* **EMILY**
>   *returns.*)

EMILY. What else can you make? Rodney, get it together,
what else can you make?

>   (*There is a tense pause while* **RODNEY**
>   *considers that question.*)

RODNEY. I can make the scallops.

>   (*They all consider this. Blackout.*)

Scene Five

> *(Two weeks later. Morning.* **HARRY** *is in the kitchen. He finds his Kikuichi knife, picks it up, puts it down. Looks around. After a moment,* **EMILY** *enters from the dining room, carrying menus.)*

EMILY. Harry.

HARRY. Hello, Emily.

EMILY. Well, this is a surprise. Did Mike know you were coming?

HARRY. I just stopped by to congratulate you on your rave.

EMILY. Congratulations to you, you should say. You're the chef. You created the meal.

HARRY. Yeah, that guy really loved my food. And, I didn't even have to do anything for it.

EMILY. What do you want me to say? Did you expect the whole place to fall apart when you so selfishly just walked off during the most important night of our lives? Were you trying to prove something? That we couldn't survive without you? Well, too bad for you, you proved the opposite. We did just fine. Business has skyrocketed. We're booking reservations three months in advance.

HARRY. We don't take reservations.

EMILY. We do now.

> *(***MIKE*** enters. He wears a great suit jacket over jeans and looks sensational.)*

MIKE. Harry! Hi. I didn't expect to see you.

HARRY. It is my restaurant.

MIKE. I've been calling you for two weeks. And you seem to have lost all interest in "our" restaurant. So no, I didn't expect to see you.

HARRY. Yeah, Emily was just explaining how nobody misses me down here.

EMILY. That is hardly what I said.

MIKE. It wouldn't be entirely untrue, though. You see the review?

HARRY. I may have glanced through it.

MIKE. Pretty nice, huh? We're getting calls from all sorts of places. Check it out: That real estate broker, owns everything down by the Barclay Center? Has a fifty-seat space opening up in two months. They want to know if we want it.

HARRY. The Russian guy? He's a gangster.

EMILY. We're not going to do it, of course. We're a boutique restaurant, with an extremely loyal clientele. We aren't looking to change our identity. Just to enhance it.

HARRY. And you did that.

EMILY. We're in process.

> (**HARRY** *looks at the menu, which he's picked up from the counter.*)

HARRY. The scallops.

EMILY. Our best seller.

HARRY. And salmon and the short ribs, and the – oh look, tofu with broccoli rabe and a miso glaze dressing, that's new. And vegan. Good for you. Good for you.

EMILY. We have people who ask for it.

HARRY. So I'm guessing you don't want me back.

MIKE. *(Laughing.)* Oh my god. This place has run like a clock for two weeks! No screaming, no whining about ingredients, no arguments about nothing – no. No, we do not want you back. We are doing quite well without you. It's fantastic without you. The food is food, without you.

HARRY. Okay.

MIKE. The salmon is still delicious. The spinach still wilts. The gnocchi still melts in your mouth.

HARRY. Okay.

MIKE. As it turns out, the painting does not need the hand of the painter.

HARRY. *(Snapping.)* I said okay!

EMILY. Let's all just take a few days to see how we want to proceed. Right now people's feelings are running high. Harry your contribution will always be honored. The scallops will always stay on the menu, I think that's clear. Your name is important. Perhaps you'll want to stay on as a consultant.

MIKE. I'm not consulting with him.

HARRY. No, you don't need me. Clearly. You've got Emily. You and Emily can consult away. But I want my name off this. You understand?

MIKE. Fine.

EMILY. Let's take this one step at a time.

HARRY. This isn't my restaurant anymore, you just said.

EMILY. The review just came out, Harry, and it is your food

HARRY. It's not my food, you just said.

EMILY. It is your food that someone else cooked but it is still your food. The review wasn't just a rave for the restaurant, it was a rave for you. I think we should all enjoy this moment and cherish it and feel great. We don't have to rush into

HARRY. So you want to take my restaurant but still use my name.

MIKE. Take your name off, no one cares!

EMILY. Of course we care!

MIKE. Take his name off, if you don't he's just going to run around and say we're using his name to legitimize our shitty food.

EMILY. We are using his name and we have earned the right to use it. I pulled in a lot of favors to get us this far and there's a lot of capital that's been sunk into this and people are not going to be happy to hear that he's pulled his name so everyone just needs to get a grip. I did what I said I was going to do and I took a restaurant that was destined to DISAPPEAR and lose its ENTIRE INVESTMENT and I turned it into a bona fide hit and you two LOSERS are not going to tear defeat out of the jaws of victory just because you're idiots. So you both can just go home now and read your rave review and enjoy it. You got what you wanted. You got what you wanted.

> (**RODNEY** *stands in the door.* **HARRY** *turns, sees him.*)

HARRY. Here he is! The man of the hour. Hello, Judas.

RODNEY. Hey, Benedict. How you been?

HARRY. You been having fun, pretending to be a chef?

RODNEY. More fun that you're having, pretending not to be.

> (**RODNEY** *goes to the pantry, reaches in and gets out a chef's apron. He puts it on.*)

EMILY. We're going to need a minute here, Rodney.

RODNEY. This is my kitchen, Emily. We got fifty people coming tonight. You really want me to go hang out in the dining room? I got to prep.

    (He gets to work.)

HARRY. This is your kitchen now?

RODNEY. It's not yours. You left.

HARRY. And you stayed.

MIKE. We all stayed. And nobody freaked out.

RODNEY. *(Correcting him.)* Emily freaked out some.

MIKE. But then she didn't. None of us did. We got the job done. And the restaurant survived.

HARRY. For now.

MIKE. For now is good enough for me.

HARRY. So you guys think you can just steal my restaurant and my kitchen and my recipes and keep using my name, and no one is going to notice that?

MIKE. They haven't yet.

HARRY. Well, that, you know – that's fantastic.

    (He laughs.)

Those fucking scallops. I was just showing off. Wow. You were right. I probably should have just given him a carrot on a plate. Sorry, I'm having a little trouble breathing right now. Oh, that would be the multiple knives I just pulled out of my back.

    (He picks up a knife from the counter and shows it to **MIKE.** **MIKE** *takes a step back.)*

MIKE. You're crazy.

HARRY. *(Calm.)* I'm not crazy, I'm angry, Mike. 'Cause let me tell you something. You Suck.

    (Then.)

This is actually going to take some time to get over.

I'm going to go get drunk now, and then I'm going to cook myself a great meal. People suck. They do suck. But food doesn't.

*(He points the knife at **MIKE**, simple, so angry he is calm.)*

You Suck.

(Then.)

But food doesn't.

(He starts to go.)

RODNEY. Jesus Harry you're such a fucking asshole.

HARRY. I'm the asshole.

RODNEY. Just say you're sorry.

HARRY. Why should I be sorry.

RODNEY. Why shouldn't you be? Don't answer that. You are sorry or you wouldn't be hanging around here, trying to get your job back.

HARRY. It's not my job. It's my creation.

RODNEY. Just say you're sorry! Who raised you anyway? Didn't your mom ever teach you how to say "sorry"?

HARRY. I'm not sorry.

RODNEY. Say it. Say it to Mike.

MIKE. I don't want him to say it.

RODNEY. I want him to say it. I want him to say it to you, and to me, and to Emily.

HARRY. To EMILY.

RODNEY. You think that takes something from you, to say sorry. You never fucking say it. You think you lose something. But all this bullshit you've been spouting?

Everything you think you know! That cost you everything. You fucking fell apart, couldn't even cook a fucking scallop. That's not because somebody stabbed you in the back. That's because you won't bow to it. You won't bow to your own talent. That's why you lost everything. You don't deserve it. Get out of my kitchen. Mike, can you see how many orders of short ribs we still got? Emily, grab me a couple of bottles of Chablis I ordered last week. I gotta prep the risotto.

> (**RODNEY** *starts to work. That really is the last word.* **MIKE** *goes back to work.* **EMILY** *goes to work.* **HARRY** *watches them. Then:*)

HARRY. I'm sorry.

> (*There is a pause.*)

I'm sorry Emily. I'm sorry, Rodney.

> (*A beat.*)

I'm sorry, Mike.

> (*They continue to ignore him.*)

I said I was sorry! Now what do you want me to do?

RODNEY. You can help prep the scallops. They're where they always are.

> (**HARRY** *goes to the refrigerator, and gets out the scallops. After a moment, he takes them to the work station. After another moment,* **MIKE** *joins him there.*)

> (*They look at the scallops together, to make sure they're good.*)

> (*Blackout.*)

End of Play